Readers love the Obsidian series by JON KEYS

Obsidian Sun

"The magic system is unique and intricate, the characters are authentic, and the world is nearly touchable it seems so real."

—Queer Sci Fi

"A new fantasy world like the one Jon Keys has created with his 'Obsidian' series is a rare delight."

—Rainbow Book Reviews

Obsidian Moons

"This book is filled with adventure, mystery, danger, and love. It was such an exciting read."

—Gay Book Reviews

"The world is vibrant and unique."

—Prism Book Alliance

By JON KEYS

Camouflage
Heart of the Pines
Home Grown
Iced
One Pulse (Dreamspinner Anthology)

OBSIDIAN SERIES
Obsidian Sun
Obsidian Moons

Published by DREAMSPINNER PRESS
www.dreamspinnerpress.com

CAMOUFLAGE

Jon Keys

Published by

DREAMSPINNER PRESS

5032 Capital Circle SW, Suite 2, PMB# 279, Tallahassee, FL 32305-7886 USA
www.dreamspinnerpress.com

Camouflage
© 2017 Jon Keys.

Cover Art
© 2017 L.C. Chase.
http://www.lcchase.com
Cover content is for illustrative purposes only and any person depicted on the cover is a model.

ISBN: 978-1-63533-232-2
Digital ISBN: 978-1-63533-233-9
Library of Congress Control Number: 2016915178
Published January 2017
v. 1.0

Printed in the United States of America
∞
This paper meets the requirements of
ANSI/NISO Z39.48-1992 (Permanence of Paper).

CHAPTER ONE

NASH FLIPPED through his closet, trying to decide what to take. He pulled out his best black silk shirt and tossed it to the bed. He'd never been to a ranch, and he'd sure never been to Oklahoma. At this point he didn't care. He'd been offered a place to chill out for a week or so. If he didn't get out of Atlanta soon, he'd end up dead.

Jimmy sifted through the pile of clothes Nash had chosen before turning to smirk at him. "Why don't you grab a handful of wifebeaters and a few pairs of ratty jeans from the thrift store? Then you can toss them when they get nasty. It's not like the hicks will notice what you're wearing."

Nash scowled at his friend. "Luke seems to be a nice guy. We've been chatting online for months. It isn't like he talked me into anything."

"You thought that about the last guy to fuck you up too. He landed you a bed in the hospital for a few days. Besides, how did you find your studly cowboy? Seems a little flaky."

"It's not the same thing at all. Luke doesn't know what I do. Which is exactly why I wanted to get to know him better. Where Luke lives sounds about as opposite of Atlanta as possible."

"Exactly! You're afraid to tell the little cowboy you're a hooker 'cause you think he's going to dump you. And he probably will."

"You know, for a best friend, you can be a real asshole sometimes."

"What do you want me to say? You think all it'll take is one *Pretty Woman* moment, and your life'll all be good."

"Knock it off. I need a break. A few days out of Atlanta will give me a chance to relax."

He turned to the closet, hoping that would end their conversation. As he stepped inside, he was surrounded with the scent of cologne and leather. He felt Jimmy's presence, and a twinge of surprise shot through Nash when there were no more comments. After a minute or

1

two, he walked out with an armload of pants and tossed them on the bed. He shot Jimmy a glance.

"What? Now you're gonna be quiet?"

Jimmy's lips narrowed to a small line. "You almost died. You know that, right?"

"I did not. I was just—beat up. That's all."

"It's been what, a month? I can still see some of the bruises."

"You said you'd help me cover those up too," he reminded Jimmy.

"I will, I will. But promise me this isn't some Oklahoma *Deliverance* boy who has a hiding place for ex-boyfriend's bodies."

Jimmy stepped closer and grabbed Nash in a hug. He returned the embrace, even as he kept his emotions under wrap. He knew what happened when you cared for people, and he'd learned it early.

"It'll be fine," Nash said. "Luke seems like a great guy. I really do need to get out of Atlanta. I can't go into a club without getting claustrophobic and feeling like I can't breathe."

Nash went to the computer and smiled at the slightly out-of-focus grinning face set as the wallpaper. "He looks like someone I could spend time with."

"He's probably a crazy-eyed psycho who's good with Photoshop."

Nash rolled his eyes and shoved Jimmy onto the bed. "It'll be fine. I'll have time to figure out what I'm going to do next." He turned away to gather the rest of his clothing and shove it into an athletic bag.

A soft snort came from Jimmy. Nash twisted to see what set him off this time. He found his friend pointing at the last few things he'd shoved into the bag. "A camo jock and cargo shorts? Damn. They wouldn't pay fifty bucks for you around here if you dressed like that."

He shrugged, pulled out a dresser drawer, and grabbed a few more things. He tried to hide the condoms by slipping them into the side pocket, but Jimmy spotted what he was doing.

His lips curled into a grin. "I thought this was just two buddies having some together time?"

"Oh shut up, would you. It's not like that."

"Well it's not like you're going to get any tricks. So you must be thinking...."

Nash glared at him from under blond eyebrows. "Let it go."

CHAPTER TWO

LUKE'S BOOTS rang out against the polished concrete floor. The incessant noise of the airport reminded him of the sound of cicadas, with none of the sense of peace, and this was a swarm of cicadas he usually tried to avoid. He checked himself again to make sure he didn't have pit stains on his starched white shirt. *I feel like I'm going to pass out. Why did I do this to myself?*

"Calm down. Why are you so nervous?"

He gave his best friend a dirty look as he ran his hands down his sides. "Chris, I'm not nervous. I want to make a good first impression."

"You two have been talking online for months. You tell me about him all the time. So relax."

"But we've never actually met. What if he can't stand me? This could be a disaster."

"Lord! Disasters are waiting around the corner for all of us. Life is full of potential disasters. Look how things went with that jerk Bobby."

Luke glanced around to see if anyone could have overheard and then frowned. "Christina Caukins, you may be my best friend, but I'd just as soon not bring up that bit of information for everyone in the dang airport to hear."

"Like anyone cares what happens in backwoods Stillwell." Chris lowered her voice. "I know you don't want to look like a backwoods hick, but this guy's flying from Atlanta to spend some time with you. That's saying something."

The sudden increase in people coming through the exit gate drew Luke's attention. He would never admit it to Chris, but he wasn't sure exactly what Nash looked like. Yes, they'd Skyped several times, but his only Internet was through a dish connection that didn't give him the clearest reception. So he was forced to analyze each young guy who looked even vaguely familiar, hoping to find Nash.

"You get any closer and you're gonna get punched," Chris said.

"Shut up. People look different on the computer screen than they do in real life."

"Tall, skinny, and blond, like the pictures he sent you," Chris said. With a grin she nodded down the aisle. "Like him."

Luke locked his gaze on the guy passing the TSA guard. It had to be Nash. Chris was right. Tall, slender, and blond. But the guy walking toward him had a lot of piercings, none of which he remembered from the pictures. The blond scruff was kind of sexy. Could this be the guy he'd talked to almost every night for the past few months? He moved closer, and Luke's chest tightened.

"Nash?"

"Luke?"

"Yeah, that's me. Glad to meet you!"

They shook hands and Luke let himself relax when Nash gave him a charming smile. The firm handshake lasted a bit longer than Luke thought absolutely necessary. As they released their grip on each other, he shot Nash a huge smile that belied his nervous tension.

"Yeah, good to meet you too." He turned to Chris and smiled at her. "And who might this pretty lady be?"

Chris held out a hand. "Christina Caukins. Most people call me Chris. I'm a friend of Luke's." She winked at Nash. "Here for moral support."

Luke knew his face turned red because it created enough heat to fry eggs. "Chris!"

"Hey, I call 'em like I see 'em." She studied Nash more closely. "Looks like you were in a brawl or something."

Nash tensed, and his eyes flicked from Chris to Luke before he answered. "No. Nothing like that. A little job-related injury. It's fine, though."

A bolt of lightning struck somewhere close and the flash lit up everything around them. A boom of thunder erupted, making the floor shake.

"Holy shit! That was close," Nash said.

"We better get going. Your plane made it in a little ahead of the storm. I'd like to miss the hailstorm they're saying we might get," Luke said.

A second bolt hit a tower. Sparks filled the sky along with an explosion so loud Nash jumped.

"We aren't going out in this, are we?"

"The worst of it is still west of us. It'll be fine. The lightning doesn't look that bad."

"It gets worse?" Nash asked, his voice higher than it had been.

"It can. But this one doesn't have a big wall cloud. We should get your stuff and hit the road."

Nash nodded and ran his hands across his shorts. "Okay. Sounds like a plan. I've got a few things in the baggage area, wherever that is."

By the time they'd retrieved Nash's luggage, the rain was coming down in buckets. "Well, shoot. It's a toad strangler," Luke said.

Nash laughed softly. "Toad strangler?"

"Yeah, you know. When it's pouring rain," Luke said.

"Okay, if you say so. But that's a new one on me."

Silence settled around them as rain sheeted down the airport windows. A crack like a high caliber rifle startled them.

"Crap. Hail." Luke glanced at the short-term parking where he'd left his truck. "I'll get the pickup and park as close to the door as I can. Hopefully we can get out of here before it gets any worse."

Without waiting for a response, he jogged to the exit. After stopping to evaluate the waterfall coming off the roof, he plunged into the summer thunderstorm. A few pieces of ice hit him as he sprinted across the flooded parking lot. He slid to a stop at the door to his pickup, almost losing his footing when the smooth soles of his boots became water skis.

He jerked open the pickup, lunged inside, and slammed the door shut behind him. A few seconds later, the diesel engine roared to life. As he worked his way out of the tiny parking spot, Chris's text tone sounded on his phone. He snatched it up and glanced at the message.

Don't get out. Just stop. We R ready. Trust Chris to have it all organized.

He eased the rumbling truck into the loading area. As he rolled to a stop, Chris and Nash sprinted through the storm. It galled him that he wasn't helping, but Chris was right. This made more sense even if it did leave him angry and frustrated.

The passenger side doors flew open. "Heads up!" Chris yelled as she tossed him Nash's carry-on case. Luke barely had time to tuck it in the backseat before an athletic bag flew in his direction. Luke tossed it on top as Nash and Chris clambered into the pickup.

They were drenched to the skin as Luke eased through the pouring rain. The trip home should be fantastic with them soaking wet and driving through a hell of a storm.

NASH GLANCED at him as they drove through the pouring rain. Luke's soaked white shirt left little to the imagination. His hairy, muscular chest and quarter-sized nipples were obvious. A gust of wind caused the truck to swerve, and Nash's attention locked on the road. The rain blew over them in sheets as the storm slammed them with hail that sounded like a thousand wild horses trying to kick their way out of a metal shed.

"Shit! This is a huge storm," Nash said.

"Yeah, seems like it got worse instead of passing over like the weatherman said. We need to get out of this hail before my truck's smashed up and we're hurt."

They raced down the interstate, barely able to see past the front of the pickup. Nash's stomach knotted as they threaded around stalled cars.

"Luke, there!" Chris pointed to an overpass a few hundred feet ahead of them.

Luke whipped the pickup sideways; a small yelp escaped Nash as a hailstone bigger than he'd ever seen bounced off the vehicle. *God, I hate storms.* The sky darkened to twilight. Luke gritted his teeth when he glanced at the vehicles swerving blindly across the interstate and shot the gaps toward the refuge. His heart pounded like a hammer as he slipped into the sheltered roadside.

Chris leaned forward with an ornery grin. "Good driving, cowboy."

Luke smiled back at her and tilted an imaginary hat. "Thank ya, ma'am. Wasn't nothing."

The storm chose that instant to intensify. Multiple bolts of lightning sliced through the sky and hail the size of baseballs ripped leaves from the trees surrounding them, bouncing several feet in the air after hitting the ground.

"Ah, crap. Look," Chris said.

Nash followed her gaze and found a couple of cars with their windshields caved in from the brutal beating given them by the hail. His jaw dropped as a semi shot past them with one corner of its windshield a spider's web of cracks.

"Is this normal?"

"No. They aren't usually this bad. This hail's going to tear up a lot of stuff," Luke said.

The wind shifted and a hailstone the size of Nash's fist bounced off the side of the pickup bed. Nash gripped the dashboard tightly when a tremor shot through the truck from a second massive hailstone.

"Dammit," Luke said under his breath.

They sat in silence while the storm howled around them. Fortunately, the torrent of hail lessened. Luke rolled down his window and peered up at the sky. "I think it's past us."

"It looks like it." Chris waved her phone in the air. "The weather app you made fun of shows the worst of the storm is already east of us."

"I didn't make fun of your phone thingy."

"You said pretty soon people won't be able to find their ass with both hands because of smartphones."

"Sometimes you could try not remembering everything I say. Besides, they don't work half the time, not at my house anyway."

Nash glanced over the seat at Chris and got a smile.

Shaking his head, Luke shifted into gear and eased onto the highway. "Okay, let's get going. It's a little over an hour drive to Stillwell."

"Really? You must live in the sticks," Nash said.

Luke glanced at Nash but locked his attention on the rain-swept road. "I told you it was in the country."

Nash's stomach knotted. "Nah, it's cool, man. I didn't realize how far out you lived. Remember, I'm in the middle of Atlanta. If I can see grass and trees, it seems country to me."

Luke's hands relaxed around the steering wheel, and he nodded. "I get that." He glanced again at Nash, and this time he grinned. "You're in for a culture shock."

Nash shrugged. "The town I grew up in wasn't that big, other than the base. But that was years ago."

Luke nodded but stayed silent while they drove through the last of the storm.

As they traveled along the rain-soaked highways, Nash studied the inside of the truck. Spotless, with every surface gleaming. Even the carpet looked new. He checked Luke out, but caught a smirk on Chris's face and decided he'd save the staring for later. He reminded himself again, this trip wasn't to find a boyfriend. Luke's place was a safe spot to crash while he figured out what he was going to do. Actually, it would be tough to get farther away from his current life than the backwoods of Oklahoma. He turned to watch the surprisingly green landscape slip past as he struggled to allow himself to relax.

"I'm getting hungry and we're close to Tahlequah. Y'all wanna stop at Sonic?" Luke asked.

"Sounds good. A cherry limeade and a burger would be amazing. How about you?" Chris asked Nash.

There was a moment of silence at the recollection of the last time he'd eaten at the Sonic in his hometown. The soldier he'd been fooling around with had taken him for a treat. He usually bought Nash a meal—after they finished. If memory served him right, about a week after his last treat at the drive-in, he was in Atlanta trying to survive on food from the dumpsters.

"Nash? Does that sound okay? Sonic's not bad. Do they have any in Atlanta?"

"Yeah, there are Sonics, just not close to where I live. Since I don't have a car…." Nash shrugged. "But I'm hungry and anything sounds delicious."

"The fried pickles are my favorite. You have to try them."

"Good Lord, woman. The way you go on about fried pickles you'd think you were pregnant. Besides, the onion rings are the best. Lots better than the pickles," Luke said.

Chris turned and stared out the window. "Pregnant. Heavens, that'll never happen. I'd have to find a guy."

Nash looked back at Chris, and she cocked her eyebrow before giving him a smile that didn't reach her eyes.

Shortly afterward they found the fast-food place and rolled to a stop at the drive-in. Luke leaned out, pushed the red button, and a crackling voice came through the speaker.

"Yeah, we want to order three number ones with cherry limeades, an order of fried pickles, and a large order of onion rings."

With another flurry of static-filled voice Nash could barely follow, the order seemed to be confirmed. Luke fished his wallet out, but Nash tapped his shoulder.

"I'll get it. It's the least I can do after you picked me up."

Their eyes met and the heat of Luke's shoulder felt good against his palm. A lump formed in his throat as he thought about the lies he'd let the rancher believe about his background. He'd had to get out of Atlanta, though, he hadn't wanted it to be someone who lived closer, and the combination made Luke's invitation too tempting.

"No, really. I want to pay for lunch." Nash tightened his grip. "Please."

Luke pursed his lips and fixed Nash in his gaze before nodding. Nash fished out his wallet and handed Luke a couple of the crisp bills he'd pulled from the ATM that morning. And he had no intention of telling anyone the transaction had drained his account.

He took the cash and studied Nash for a few seconds before he nodded. "This is the last time I'm letting you pay, though. I invited you."

Nash tapped Luke's bicep with his fist. "Like I said, I needed a break. This will be perfect."

The group sat in silence until Chris leaned forward and tapped Nash's shoulder. "So, when are you two gonna kiss? That's why I'm here. I want to see Luke finally get a nice hot kiss."

Luke's face turned so red Nash thought he'd burst into flames. "Chris! Knock it off! I told you Nash and I are just friends."

"Hey, I just want Bobby to see what he lost."

"Chris! Shut up!"

The muscles in Luke's jaw knotted and coiled.

He's not embarrassed anymore, he's pissed.

"Who's Bobby?" Nash asked.

"An ex. It's a long, ugly story," Chris said.

Tension grew until it frazzled Nash's nerves. Luke's lips were nothing but a thin slash across his face as he glared out the window while they waited. Nash glanced behind them, relieved to see a guy coming with their food.

"Hello. How are y'all today?"

The carhop's arrival broke the festering tension. Nash breathed a sigh of relief as the smiling young man began handing bags through the open window. "Does that look like everything?"

Luke glanced into the sacks. "Yup, looks good. Thanks." He took the last limeade, handed the kid a tip, and got a huge smile in return.

"If you need anything else, push the button," the carhop said.

"Thanks. We appreciate that."

The carhop left and soon everyone had a burger in their hands, inhaling their food.

Nash finished his meal and was licking the last remnants from his fingers as he said, "That was delicious. Thanks for stopping."

"No problem. They have my favorite burgers." Luke smeared ketchup over a thick onion ring and bit out a chunk. "I love their rings too. They're the best." He held out the paper sack to Nash. "Try one."

Nash fished one of Luke's treasured rings from the bag and took a bite. "Not bad." He bit off another chunk and grinned at the other two. "Really good, actually."

"See, I told you. Their onion rings rock."

"Whatever," Chris said. "He hasn't even tried the pickles."

Nash sat back, enjoying a full stomach while he listened to two people who obviously knew each other well. But they refused to let him sit quietly.

11

"You liked the onion rings, didn't you? Come on, Nash, tell me I'm right," Luke said.

"Yeah, they were pretty good. I'm not sure I'm that great of a judge, though."

Luke swung his arm over his head and whooped. "Yeah buddy! I told you he had good tastes."

"Obviously he has good tastes. He came here to see you."

Both Nash and Luke blushed, but Chris wasn't finished.

"Here. Taste a pickle. They'll knock your socks off."

Nash hesitantly lifted a hand to the tray of dill pickle slices that had been breaded and deep-fried until they were golden brown. He picked one from the pile and lifted it to his mouth.

"No! Wait. You need ranch dressing," Chris said.

"What?"

"Ranch dressing. Here." Chris held out a small container filled with white sauce. He hesitated before dunking the pickle, then slipped it into his mouth.

He chewed for a few moments, surprised that he was enjoying the combination of salty and tart with the creamy dressing. Nash grinned at Chris. "The pickle was good too. But different. I think it's a tie."

"Oh, no fair! You're siding with the girl!"

"He isn't going to get lucky with me later. So I'm thinking the man is being honest."

Luke snorted but locked his eyes on the highway. "Knock it off, Chris."

She gave him a melodramatic eye roll before crossing her arms and relaxing against the seat. In less time than he'd have thought possible, they finished off the food and were nursing the last of their drinks.

"That should hold us until dinner. I was starved," Luke said.

Nash enjoyed the tree-lined streets as they headed east and soon left the quiet town. They'd traveled a few miles when Nash's curiosity got the best of him. "I thought it'd be flat, like really flat. It's actually pretty hilly."

"We're on the western edge of the Ozarks. Some places are pretty rugged, and we have trees."

Nash grinned. "You do have trees, but nothing like the ones we have in Georgia."

Luke glanced at him and grinned. "Okay, maybe not like your pine forests, but still, there are trees. It's not like western Oklahoma."

Chris leaned between the seats, a twinkle in her eyes as she looked at Nash. "You're in dangerous territory. He's about to start preaching."

A chill rippled up Nash's back. "Preaching?"

Luke scowled at Chris. "You really aren't making brownie points today." He sat silent for a while, and Nash decided Luke had said everything he intended. But then he was off again. "I love living here, and I love this state. I know some places call it the buckle of the Bible Belt, but I like the people here. Well, at least most of them. The farm I live on was where my grandparents raised me. I inherited it when they passed away, which upset some of the family. So yeah, if you talk about this part of Oklahoma being a bad place, I get defensive."

Tension uncoiled in Nash. "I get that. Everyone should have some place to feel safe."

Luke chuckled softly and the nerves lessened. "I dunno. I live miles from town, by myself, and have a few questionable neighbors. Safe might not be what I'd call it."

Nash's chest tightened. *Am I living out a scene from* Deliverance?

Then Chris patted him on the shoulder and laughed. "Don't buy it. The only time he's lived away from here was during college. Most of the time he forgets to even lock the door. Luke likes a bit of drama, that's all."

He stuck his tongue out at Chris. "You know I could have left you at home. And I'm starting to think I should have."

She grabbed Luke's shoulder and shook it before turning it loose and giving him a little slap on the arm. "You couldn't live without me."

"I might be willing to give it a shot."

"So what's first on the agenda?" Nash asked in an effort to change the conversation.

"I thought I'd take Miss Loudmouth home, then run by the house, drop your stuff off, and check everything before we get some supper."

"That sounds good. How much farther?"

Luke smiled and flipped on his blinker. "We're at Chris's now."

It only took a minute to drop her off, and then they headed out of town. Neither of them seemed to know what to say. Usually they were chatting nonstop when they were on the computer. But now that they were within touching distance, it was as if they were strangers. Luke slowed the pickup and turned off the state highway onto a gravel road lined with trees and no signs of people. The lane wound its way through a series of hairpin turns and steep hills as they traveled deeper into the forest.

Nash looked up when they turned from the gravel road onto a narrow driveway that disappeared around another dense stand of trees. One turn later, they parked in front of a neat white frame house with a porch that wrapped around two sides. The yard was lovingly cared for, and irises of every color edged the porch. A variety of matching buildings sat on the opposite side of the road along with what looked like a maze of tall white fences made from stout metal pipe. Nash wouldn't have considered it luxurious, but a sense of comfort flowed over him. He glanced over to find Luke watching.

"Well. This is it," Luke said.

"It's cute."

Luke shrugged. "I don't know how cute it is. But it's home." He crawled out of the pickup, opened the back door, and started hauling Nash's bags toward the house.

Nash raced to catch up and reached down to grab some of the luggage. "Here. You don't have to carry my stuff for me."

Luke stopped and stood frozen in place. Then he slowly turned to Nash and a shy smile appeared. "I want you to enjoy yourself, and I'm kind of nervous. I know I live in the middle of nowhere, and it's nothing like you're used to. To make matters worse, I wasn't kidding: cell phone reception is awful. Sometimes it doesn't work at all. Sorry."

Nash sat his bag on the walkway, stepped close to Luke, and gripped him by his shoulders. He was surprised at the tingle that ran through his body but quickly recovered. "It's okay. I'm kinda nervous too. The phone's not a big deal. We've been chatting for a long time and know a lot about each other. Take it slow and everything will be fine."

He held Luke until he felt him pull away, then released his grip. He stepped back and Luke nodded. With hesitancy in his voice, he began to talk. "I know it'll be fine. It's just…. Well, this is kind of different. Having you here."

Nash chuckled and dove in for a quick hug. "I'm pretty low maintenance. Relax."

A smile crept across Luke's face. "Come on. Let's get you settled and then we'll grab some supper."

They walked into a living room that was as immaculate as Luke's pickup. The comfortable chairs were as inviting as the house itself. The major difference was the furniture had obviously been chosen by Luke. The brown leather couch and recliner set a comforting tone replicated by most of the pieces around the room. As he glanced about, Nash stopped to admire the landscape photographs covering one wall.

"They're mine. I took them around here and down at Tenkiller. Just a stupid hobby to keep me outta trouble," Luke said.

"They're really good. The compositions are great." Nash turned to Luke. "What's Tenkiller?"

"The lake that's close. Maybe we'll go camping while you're here. Come on, let me show you your bedroom."

He walked down the hallway but stopped about halfway and turned to Nash. "I hope this is okay. I don't have many overnight guests."

"I'm sure it'll be fine. I'm really not that picky. Your house is a lot nicer than the apartment where I live." He grinned at Luke. "You're going to spoil me. Then I'll never want to leave."

Luke paled, and his Adam's apple wiggled back and forth several times. After a short pause, Luke started down the hall again, opened the last door, and walked through.

The room screamed high school athlete with its collection of photos and newspaper clippings. A few helmets and singlets were on display. Sprinkled in with all the sports memorabilia were framed photos of Luke showing cattle. Nash turned slowly, taking in the world of a younger Luke.

"I know. It was my room and since I use the master bedroom now, and never have visitors, I've pretty much left it alone. My grandmother kept everything and plastered it on my walls. Some of this was in the living room, and I've moved it in here so it looks less like the Luke Memorial."

"Was there anything you didn't do in high school?"

"It's not that bad. I showed cattle and wrestled. Those were enough."

"These are of you in a singlet?"

"Yup, those are me."

"Still have them?"

"Yeah, somewhere. Why?"

"Maybe you'll have to put them on and show me some of your moves." He winked at Luke.

He turned so red Nash swore his face would glow in the dark. He laid Nash's bag on the bed. "Yeah, okay, ah. I'll let you change if you want. We can head back to town in an hour or so. I thought we'd hit the barbecue place but they close at eight, so we need to go pretty soon."

"Barbecue sounds good. What do I need to wear?"

Luke grinned. "I think you have to wear a shirt. Probably shoes too. It'd be good if you didn't have holes in your jeans so your junk shows. Otherwise about anything will work."

"Got it. I didn't want to be underdressed."

"There's no fancy places in Stillwell. You're safe. I'll go change and get ready. The downpour at the airport left me feeling like a drowned rat."

"Okay. See you in a bit."

CHAPTER THREE

NASH WATCHED Luke as they drove down the road toward town. He'd looked good at the airport, at least what Nash could remember before Luke ran through the pouring rain, but once he cleaned up he was outstanding. The pullover shirt tapered to his hips, and Nash licked his lips in appreciation. *Even more importantly, he seems like a nice guy. Not that I'm a great judge.*

"So what do you think?"

Nash jumped, afraid he'd been busted. But he realized the question wasn't what he'd thought when Luke motioned at the scenery that rolled past.

"The house is cool. I mean, you have all that space to yourself. It's so quiet too. I don't know how I'm going to sleep without sirens and squealing brakes."

Luke fixed his eyes on the road ahead, his knuckles white on the steering wheel. "Yeah. It's quiet most of the time."

"Sorry. I forgot how you got it."

"It's okay. I just miss them a lot."

Nash reached over, patted Luke's leg, and gave it a squeeze. "Sorry, but at least you had someone who loved you."

Luke started to say something, but Nash interrupted, not wanting him to get too inquisitive. "So, we're going for barbecue? I love pulled pork."

"This might be more Texas barbecue than you're used to. I always get the brisket."

"And you like their fries, right?"

Luke glanced over at him. "How did you know that?"

"Oh I don't know, maybe because you told me one night when we were chatting."

Luke relaxed his grip on the wheel and a grin appeared. "Oh. Yeah, I guess I did." He looked over to Nash and then refocused on the road. "Makes me wonder what else I've told you and forgot."

Nash chuckled and twisted in the seat so he faced Luke. "Let's see. You like corn dogs with mustard and ketchup, which is disgusting. You also like to rope, but you can't help but worry about the calves sometimes. What else…."

"Okay, okay. You've made your point. Enough Luke stories. And why don't I know any of your embarrassing habits?"

Nash's relaxed moment faded, and he turned back to the wall of trees they were driving through. "Nothing worth sharing. Especially nothing as cute as how you got the crescent-shaped scar on your butt."

"There was nothing cute about that. The damn dog was trying to kill me."

"It's the owner's fault. They make the dogs mean."

"Whatever. The owner didn't bite me."

They drove the rest of the way in silence. The typical small-town business staples rolled past as they got closer to their destination. *Looks familiar, a lifetime and a thousand miles ago.*

"You hungry?" Luke asked.

Nash's stomach picked that point to rumble. "From that sound, you'd think I was about to starve."

"Good, 'cause we're here." Luke turned into the parking lot as Nash checked out the low-slung building with its simple "BBQ" sign in front. As Luke searched for a parking spot, Nash inhaled the hickory-smoke-laden air. When they rounded the back of the place, Nash spotted the monstrous black behemoth filling the area with the scent of meats of every kind.

They found a place to park and made their way inside. Luke threaded his way to the counter with Nash close behind. A smiling woman with her blonde hair pulled back motioned them closer. "What sounds good tonight, Luke?" she asked.

"I think a couple of the sampler plates and two sweet teas."

She looked knowingly at Nash. "And fries. He always has fries."

Luke grinned and shrugged. "Guilty. They're the best."

The woman motioned toward an empty table. "Grab a seat and I'll bring it out to you."

A short time later Nash had both elbows propped on the table and was halfway through a side of ribs. "You were right. The hot barbecue sauce is killer."

Luke swallowed the piece of brisket he was working on and looked at Nash. "Told you. The beans are great too. The place isn't fancy, but it's delicious food."

Nash pulled off another rib and gnawed it like an ear of corn. The food was good, but he thought the company was better. Feeling a little ornery, he leaned closer to Luke, making smacking noises, knowing his face was smeared with sauce.

"Hey, what'd you think? Want some of this?"

With a nervous laugh, Luke glanced around them. "Knock it off, you goof. You've got barbecue all over you."

Nash gathered up a few paper towels and wiped his face. After considering Luke, he leaned across the table. "You okay? If me teasing around is making you uncomfortable…."

"No, it's okay. I don't mind."

"Then what's making you so uptight?"

"They might think it's more than friends out for barbecue. I haven't really been out with anyone before."

"You've never been on a date?"

"Not really. I went out a few times in college, but not since coming back." Luke paused and glanced at Nash before he continued. "Yeah, nothing I'd call a date.

"You've been out of college for a while. How could you not date? I thought you were out."

"Oh, they know, but you know little towns and all their crap. It's—" Luke stopped, and his eyes locked on the business's door as it swung open.

Nash wondered what was going on when a mass of people swept through the entrance. They all seemed loud and excited. He watched closely and turned to Luke. "What's going on? Did everyone get their egg money at once?"

"The high school football team had an out-of-season scrimmage, and it looks like it's over. Football is more important than money, at least around here."

Nash watched the crowd for a few more seconds before he shrugged. "Doesn't take much to get some people worked up, I guess."

"No, it doesn't." Luke glanced at the crowd again, and he went rigid.

Nash looked again but couldn't see anything more than the same milling throng. "What's wrong?"

"Not a big deal. You ready to go? We could stop for some ice cream at—"

Nash laid his hands on top of one of Luke's. "You might as well tell me. I'm going to worm it out of you eventually anyway, even if it takes liquor."

Luke sighed deeply. "I suppose. It's not like I'll be able to avoid him the whole time you're here."

Nash waited for Luke to continue, but he realized more information wasn't going to happen soon if he didn't help it along. So he gave it another shot. "He who? What's going on? You know you can talk to me. Hell, if it's making you nervous, text it to me."

"Yeah, apparently I'm a blabbermouth around you. So, you might as well know. My sort of ex just walked in. Long story."

"Your ex? I thought…."

"Like I said, it's complicated. Do you mind if we go somewhere else for dessert?"

Nash considered saying something, then decided against it. Instead he looked over the people, trying to decide which one was Luke's former lover. His curiosity got the best of him. "Which one?"

"The blond guy with the red shirt that says 'Stillwell Indians.'"

Nash started chuckling. "You're kidding me, right? They're all wearing a red Indians jersey."

"Him. The guy in the corner…."

Nash looked again, and this time immediately spotted who Luke must be talking about. Almost as tall as Nash, but with the build of a fading high school football star. He was at the center of the mob of men waiting by the door and talking loudly.

Nash glanced at Luke. "The big blond guy everyone seems to want to talk to?"

"Yeah. His name's Bobby. Robert Doyle."

Nash glanced again. There was something familiar about the guy. He was certain they'd met before. He'd figure it out at some point. Could he be a trick? Nash tried to forget their faces. Tried, anyway. But this guy seemed familiar.

"If you don't mind." Luke nodded toward the door.

Nudged from his own thoughts, Nash started sliding out of the booth. "Yeah, sure. Sounds like someone to avoid."

"He's the town's football hero, a bank loan officer, and pretty much everyone's darling. Between the two of us… let's say things ended badly on several fronts."

As they made their way to the door, Nash heard a booming voice from across the room. "Hey, Luke!" They stopped and Bobby walked over to them.

"Luke! Long time no see." Bobby stuck out his hand.

Luke's face hardened as they shook hands. Nash was impressed, though; Luke seemed to be keeping it under wraps, for the most part. Then the ex-jock turned to Nash and extended a hand. "Hey, I don't think we've met. I'm Bobby, Bobby Doyle."

It was the voice, the movement, something. He was so familiar. "Nice to meet you, Bobby. I'm Nash Gallo."

The handshake was firm, one that you'd get from someone who needed to give you the impression they cared, but only the impression. Like a used car salesman or someone peddling insurance… or an underhanded banker.

Bobby turned to Luke, grabbed his shoulder, and squeezed it in a gesture far too familiar for the look etched on Luke's face. "Hey, good to see you again. Don't be a stranger. Stop in the bank sometime and we can grab lunch or something." He turned his attention to Nash. "It was good to meet you too. Hope you boys have fun." He winked before turning to rejoin the crowd. As he did a little blonde girl in pigtails ran up and tugged at his arm. Bobby lifted her to his hip and held her with one arm wrapped around her tiny waist.

A woman with all the signs of being a trophy wife walked beside him and kissed Bobby's cheek. Another young girl held the woman's hand. Hurt and anger flicked across Luke's face before he shot out the door without another word.

That went well.

LUKE JUMPED into the pickup, seething that he'd let Bobby play him again. He'd looked like a complete loser. As Nash buckled himself in, Luke fired up the truck and roared out of the parking lot. They bounced through a few healthy potholes and slid onto a city street.

He clenched his teeth as his jaw muscle knotted. "Sorry. I didn't know he'd be there."

Nash sat quietly as they raced around another corner. When gravel sprayed from the tires on the third turn, Nash laid his hand on Luke's arm. "I think we should stop and talk. If you don't want to talk, that's cool too, but I don't think my nerves can take a faster corner."

Luke glanced at Nash and deflated. "Sorry. I'm acting like a little kid who didn't get his way."

"No. You look like a person who's been hurt badly. Do you want to talk about it?"

Luke shrugged, his stomach knotting as he struggled to decide what to do. Nash remained silent while they traveled a few more blocks before turning into a city park. Luke sat staring at the green space and never turned to Nash, whose apprehension was probably growing with each heartbeat. He knew they should talk about it now, even if that was the last thing he wanted to do. With another twist of his gut, Luke asked, "So what do you want to know? I'm sure you figured out most of it."

Nash shrugged. "I don't know that I've figured out anything. But I think you need someone to listen. This is one thing you haven't told me about."

He studied Nash, the feelings inside him roiling at the necessity of having a discussion about Bobby so soon. But he calmed himself. The last thing he wanted was to look like even more of a loser.

"What can I say? I was the one Bobby cheated on his wife with and was stupid enough to keep doing it when I should have stopped years ago. It started after I came home from college."

"Crap happens, more than we'd like to think. You can do better, though, if you asked me. He comes across as a two-timing asshole."

Luke slumped against the seat without meeting Nash's gaze. "I can't believe I'm such a chump. He'd call, say he could meet, and I'd go wherever he said."

"And what happened?"

"For years he kept saying he was leaving Aimee. But she kept shelling out kids. Then a few months ago, I got fed up and realized he was never going to leave her. I really didn't want to be the bad guy who hurt those two little girls either. So I broke it off with him."

"And then what happened?"

He gave Nash a significant look. "I crawled in my little hole for a month or so to do the poor-me routine. I checked out a few dating sites. The rest you can figure out since you're here."

Nash leaned close and patted him on the back. His spicy scent filled the truck, and Luke wanted to wrap his arms around the handsome man beside him and give him a lust-filled kiss. Luke shuddered, realizing he was doing it again. *I'm telling him about what a disaster my life is and I'm getting horny. What am I, some kind of perv?*

They separated slowly, and all Luke could hear was his own heavy breathing. Nash squeezed his shoulder before settling back into the seat. His touch sent jolts through Luke, and his cock stiffened.

"I think things will work out." Nash jarred him back to their conversation.

Luke felt like he had a spring sunburn as heat traveled up his neck and across his cheeks. He let his knotted muscles relax as he studied the man next to him. After spending a few seconds pulling himself together, he still thought his voice sounded squeaky when he spoke.

"I hope you're right. You still up for the ice cream? We can get shakes at Sonic. They have a bunch of flavors and stuff."

Never breaking their eye contact, Nash smiled. "Sure. Whatever sounds good to you."

A short time later they were on the highway to the ranch. Luke noticed the limitations of his hometown more than ever before. Tonight people he'd known his entire life seemed judgmental. It wasn't much—a glance here, a few whispers there—but it left Luke nauseous.

"Sorry about tonight. I know it's kind of boring around here and tonight's drama didn't help. But I need to get home and check on the animals. Maybe tomorrow we can go to Tahlequah and look around, or Muskogee. Sorry, but it's kind of backwoods around here."

Nash smiled at Luke as he sucked on the drink straw. After a few sips he began again. "I came here to see you. I know you have responsibilities. If you want to go somewhere else, I'm okay with that. I needed a break, and this still seems like a great place to unwind."

Heat rose up Luke's neck and he felt certain he was beet red again. "We'll do some fun stuff. Maybe camp out one night at Tenkiller. I don't want you bored to death."

"I'm fine, Luke. Relax."

Luke smiled as they turned into the driveway and wound their way to the front of the house. Luke turned off the engine and slumped in his seat. His gaze locked ahead of him for several seconds before he turned to Nash. "I guess I'm being stupid, but I've never had someone around. I need to check the cows, take care of the horses and my mule. You can go with me if you'd like. Or you can chill out at the house. I have satellite TV and it's decent. Maybe a nap. I'm sure you're tired."

"I'd love to go with you. I just need to change into some shorts."

"Umm, you might want jeans. We have to walk through some pretty rough pastures."

"Jeans it is, then."

AN HOUR or so later found them back at the house, having taken care of Luke's livestock. Nash had been happy to tag along, helping when he could. It was all new to him, and he followed Luke's instructions, or mimicked him when there weren't any.

"So. Now you've seen the ranch."

"Pretty cool. I've mostly lived in town. There's not much livestock in Atlanta."

"My place actually is pretty small. But it supported my grandparents. I'm hoping I can make a living at it too." A dark expression settled on Luke. "If something doesn't happen to screw everything up."

He turned to Nash with a forced smile. "Enough of that crap. You want a snack? I could make us some popcorn, and we could watch TV. If that sounds…."

"Luke, that sounds great. Relax. You don't have to keep me entertained every minute I'm here."

"Okay, okay. Got it." Luke rummaged in the cabinet, emerging with a pan and lid. Nash leaned against the door as Luke started making them some stovetop popcorn. It wasn't long before it sounded like an army assault as the kernels exploded. A minute or so later, Luke dumped the finished popcorn into a bowl for them to share.

Nash leaned over, grabbed a handful of fresh popcorn, and tossed it in his mouth. He chewed, enjoying the flavor much more than he expected. "This is really good. I'd have been fine with nuked popcorn, but I can't remember having any this tasty before."

"A roommate I had in college showed me how to make it. I can't eat the microwave stuff now."

Nash munched on another handful of the crunchy treat. Luke handed him the bowl, moved into the kitchen, and opened the refrigerator door. "What do you want to drink? I have coke and beer."

"A beer'd be fine."

Luke grabbed two bottles, then motioned toward the living room. He slipped ahead and sat in an overstuffed chair as Nash settled on the leather couch. He looked at Luke and cocked his head. "It's going to be tough to share the popcorn if you're all the way over there."

Luke blushed again, and Nash couldn't keep from grinning. *Man, he's easily flustered.*

"Sure. Makes sense." He moved to the couch, sat beside Nash, and started flipping channels.

"Wait! What was that? Flip back a couple of channels."

Luke glanced at Nash but did as he was asked.

"There. That one."

On the screen was an almost empty warehouse with people making sculptures. Nash smiled at the confused look on Luke's face. "Yeah, I know it's stupid. But they're people who want to do special effects makeup. I always thought I'd like to take some art classes. I was pretty good at it, but my parents thought it was useless, and then I moved to Atlanta." Nash shrugged and leaned against the arm of the couch. "We can watch something else. I spotted it as it went past."

"No, this is fine. It looks interesting. I always wondered how they made those things. But I can't draw a straight line, so I'm pretty hopeless at making art."

"My high school art teacher always said if you want a straight line, use a ruler. But I get what you mean."

Luke handed him a beer, and they settled the popcorn between them. Before long, Nash leaned toward the screen, engrossed in the program. He glanced over to find Luke grinning at him.

"What?"

"You're so intense."

Nash flushed with embarrassment as he became flustered. "I just…. It's kind of cool. The show, you know."

"You should take some classes. I'm sure there are tons of schools in Atlanta that teach art."

Nash hoped his disappointment didn't show as he turned back to the program. A minute later, he felt a nudge against his arm. "Hey, you could go to school, you know. I bet you'd be outstanding."

"Can't. Not right now, anyway."

"But it's something—"

"No." The darkness that was such a part of his life closed in around Nash. He exhaled slowly through his nose and took a minute to get his emotions under control. He plastered a grin on his face and turned to Luke. He didn't feel like smiling, but he hoped Luke couldn't tell. "Let's watch the show, okay?"

Luke nodded but looked apprehensive. Nash leaned against the back of the couch, but the evening wasn't as relaxed as it had been earlier. After a little while, Nash reached over and pulled Luke against him. Luke tensed but didn't resist. He moved the bowl from between them and draped his arm over Luke's shoulder. He rubbed his chin over the shorter man's head until Luke chuckled and pushed Nash away. "Knock it off, you brute. That tickles."

Nash took a couple of drinks of his beer and waited until Luke relaxed next to him. He leaned down, put his lips against Luke's ear, and burped.

"Eww! Nasty!" Luke lurched up, rubbing his ear against his shirt. "That was gross."

Laughter bubbled up from inside Nash and he burped again. "I have no idea what you're talking about."

"Oh really?" Luke dove on Nash, pinned him against the couch, and dug his fingers into Nash's ribs.

Nash burst into laughter as he tried to escape. "Come on. Knock it off. That tickles!"

Luke worked his fingers higher until Nash gasped for air between laughs. "I give. I give. Come on, stop."

"You going to burp in my ear again?"

Nash became mischievous and a little giddy to think he might have found someone he could relax around. He decided to chance it and smiled at Luke. "Maybe."

"Oh, you think?" Luke dug his fingers into Nash's armpits and started tickling him again.

"Stop! Stop," Nash gasped out between breaths as the waves of hysterical laughter overwhelmed him. He was helpless to deal with the tickling. He might be taller than Luke, but he lacked Luke's muscle. Luke stopped with a twinkle in his eyes and a smirk on his lips.

"You going to be good now?"

"Oh, I don't think you want me to be too good," Nash said.

"I have no idea what you're talking about. How about we finish your show and relax before we hit the sack."

"I like that idea." He settled onto the couch and pulled Luke back against him. Any tension between them evaporated. By the time they'd sat through the local news, Luke began to yawn.

"Sorry. I guess I'm a party pooper."

"Don't sweat it. I'm pretty tired too." He patted Luke's back. "Thanks for a great day, and a fun night."

Luke's expression became more somber. "Oh, I'm sure it was impressive."

Nash cradled Luke's face in his hands and turned it so their gazes locked. "It was a good day. The best I've had in a long time. I can't remember laughing this much in forever."

An impish expression came over Luke. "It was all the tickling."

"Oh yeah, I'm sure tickling me until I couldn't breathe was it."

They moved away from each other, but then their eyes caught. An awkward dance happened before Nash took over. Without a word he pulled Luke into a tight embrace and pressed their lips together.

Luke resisted at first, the impetuous kiss clearly startling him. He could have easily stopped Nash if he'd wished. Nash ran his hands over Luke's muscular back, enjoying the heat radiating against his palms. He felt Luke move away and lifted his hands free. Nash took a moment, shocked he'd done what he promised himself he wouldn't. Not with this man and not on this trip.

Nash met Luke's gaze as the heat built. "I.... Sorry. I really wasn't planning that."

Luke touched his lips as if they had been burned. He shook his head and nodded at Nash. "Yeah. Kinda surprised me. I...."

"Yeah, I know. Don't sweat it. Let me help clean up."

Nash picked up their dishes and headed for the kitchen. Luke's eyes were on him as he walked into the adjacent room. Once he'd put them in the sink, he turned to find Luke right behind him.

"I guess I'll get some sleep. It's been a long day," Nash said.

Luke nodded, but Nash could see the tension in the way he held himself. He gave Luke some time to recover before patting him on the shoulder. "Night."

He still appeared dumbstruck as Nash smiled at him and headed to the guest bedroom. *I wonder how much that little stunt cost me.*

CHAPTER FOUR

NASH DRIFTED awake, taking a minute to remember he wasn't in Atlanta. He hadn't slipped out of some hotel room in the middle of the night. Stretching, he enjoyed the crisp white sheets that felt so luxurious against his bare skin. As the morning sunshine filled the room, he lay quiet, enjoying the fresh breeze through the window beside his bed and the soothing sounds of Luke's animals.

He glanced at the clock as the sound of someone being industrious drifted from the kitchen. Eight fifteen. *Damn, I never wake up before noon.* Soon the smell of bacon drifted into the room and Nash's stomach urged him out of bed.

He moved toward the doorway, then remembered he was naked. It probably wouldn't be the best idea to wander through the house without wearing a stitch of clothing, especially after surprising Luke with a kiss last night. Nash still wasn't certain how that happened. He pulled his bag out of the closet and dug through the clothes until he found a loose-fitting pair of athletic shorts and pulled them on. He adjusted his equipment before moving down the hallway.

When he walked into the kitchen, Luke's smiling face greeted him. "There you are. I thought you were going to sleep all day. I'm fixing us some breakfast. I thought we'd go camping today. Down to Lake Tenkiller."

The torrent of words left Nash frozen in place, trying to sort through what Luke said. He gave up and glanced around the kitchen. "Coffee?"

Luke chuckled and pointed to the coffeemaker. "Help yourself. There's a carton of cream in the fridge and the sugar's in the pantry if you need it."

"I take it black, but thanks."

Luke went back to turning the bacon while Nash filled his cup. He brought it to his nose and inhaled deeply before he took a sip. *Ah, smells good.* His senses filled with the taste of strong coffee. *Not bad, had worse, much worse.* He walked over to see what Luke was doing.

"You might not want to come too close. The bacon's popping all over creation this morning."

Nash sipped a little more coffee, and the cobwebs worked their way out of his head. "Smells delicious."

"I'm not much of a cook. My grandmother was pretty old-fashioned about who did what, so I never learned to feed myself until college. But I can make bacon and eggs. I got a couple dozen from the neighbor yesterday so we'd have fresh eggs if we wanted them."

"Bacon and eggs sounds yummy. But that's a lot of bacon."

"It's not all for breakfast. I cooked extra to take with us. I love BLTs, especially when I'm camping."

"Camping sounds fun, especially with some good food. You said there was a lake not far away?"

"Yeah, about ten or fifteen miles. I thought you would enjoy it. It's kinda warm this time of year, but I know some spots where we can jump in the water, lounge around, roast wieners, and set some marshmallows on fire."

"Sounds like a blast. But what about your animals?"

"The cattle will be fine for one night. Chris said she'd take care of the horses and Jack. So it's all set."

Nash jumped onto the counter, folded his legs underneath him, and settled in to watch Luke make breakfast. The oven timer rang, and Luke looked around. "Where'd I put that dish cloth?"

Nash slid off the counter, slipped the towel from Luke's shoulder, and pulled a pan of biscuits from the oven.

"They look good," Nash said as Luke flashed him a frown.

"Don't be too impressed. They're whomp 'em biscuits."

"What?"

"You know, they come in a tube and you whomp them against the counter to open."

31

Nash chuckled as he set the pan on the counter while Luke filled their plates. A few minutes later they were enjoying one of the best breakfasts he could remember. But he didn't see morning very often either. After dragging his buttered biscuit through the last bit of egg on his plate, he slipped it into his mouth, then grinned at Luke as he swallowed.

"That was outstanding. The whomp 'em biscuits were perfect."

"Whatever. At least I didn't burn them."

"So what needs to be done before we take off?"

"I need to check the horses, and we can pull out the camping stuff. We should be able to get there around noon."

Nash warmed to the subject, but something else occurred to him. "I didn't bring swim trunks. Can we go somewhere I can get a suit?"

Luke studied him. "I bet I have one small enough for you, unless you'd rather get a new one."

Nash smirked at the thought of his small butt in a suit that fit Luke. But it would save him a few bucks, and he wasn't exactly making money while he was on vacation. "Sure, that'd be fine. I might need to borrow a piece of rope, though."

"Oh, give me a break. I'm not that fat."

"I'm not seeing fat, dude. Just a rocking bubble butt." Nash filled with an attraction he hadn't experienced in years when Luke ducked his head and blushed. *He's so cute.*

LUKE TRIED to relax as he drove them to a remote spot only a few steps from the lake. The four-wheel drive pickup growled softly as it crept up and down the steep hill that the almost invisible road ran through. The strong smell of cedar drifted into the cab through Luke's open window as a branch was crushed under the tire.

They topped a final hill and the trees gave way to a cozy opening with a view of sparkling blue water that filled the horizon. Luke coasted into a spot that had obviously been used as a campsite for years and stopped the truck. "What'd you think?"

"Looks secluded. Is this when I find out you're a sex addict and you've brought me out here to have your way with me?"

Luke felt his face ignite. "No, nothing like that."

"Too bad."

Luke's skin got even hotter, which he hadn't thought possible. He stammered a few times, trying to say something. His gut twisted in knots as he struggled for a response. Nash squeezed his shoulder, then pulled him close and gave him a peck on the cheek.

"I'm teasing. You're way too nice a guy to screw me like a baboon."

"Really? You never know," Luke said, and immediately wished he hadn't.

Nash looked stunned. Then his expression cracked and he laughed. "Maybe later we can see about the hot monkey sex thing."

Luke joined his laughter and the tension evaporated. "Maybe the monkeys should put up the tent and get something to eat. I don't know about you, but I'm starved."

"Sounds like a plan." Nash vaulted out of the pickup and soon the two of them had the tent set up and were making inroads into the cooler of food Luke packed.

"The BLTs are pretty good. Maybe I'm just hungry, but everything tastes excellent," Nash said.

"I told you we'd use all the bacon I fixed."

Luke took another bite of his sandwich and studied Nash from behind it. He fought down the flustered feeling and tried to focus on their lunch. Why was he letting all this get to him, and what was the teasing about sex earlier? He wasn't ready to deal with it. Although, Nash was only here for a short time, and he was really cute. He looked out at the lake, then at Nash. "It's pretty hot. I'll clean up the lunch crap, and we can go for a swim."

"Excellent idea. I know I'm hotter than a popcorn fart."

Luke chuckled again. "I didn't know popcorn could fart."

"Oh yeah. They're gassy little shits."

Luke shook his head, a grin splitting his face as he cleaned up from their lunch. Nash pitched in to help, and they soon had everything stored away. Luke disappeared into the tent and emerged a few seconds later with a couple of towels. Nash took one look at what was in Luke's hands and started laughing.

"Really? You have camo towels?"

Luke grinned. He'd picked them on purpose. "Of course. I found them online and ordered a whole set."

"You a big-time hunter or something?"

"Not anymore. I don't have time. But I liked to hunt quail and deer when I was in high school. Some of my buddies called me Camo."

"I think I'll stick with Luke if that's okay with you."

"Actually, I'd prefer it. I think I'm too old for nicknames." Luke dug through the wad of clothing on his arm and tossed Nash a deep red pair of shorts. "These are too small for me. I thought they'd fit you, though."

Nash held them up and lifted one eyebrow. Without a word, he unbuttoned his cargo shorts and let them fall to the ground. Luke's jaw dropped to see Nash standing naked from the waist down for the world to see. But despite the shock, he was riveted by the soft cock with the thick ring through its tip, and his low-hanging balls. Nash stepped into the swimsuit, and Luke swallowed hard as Nash's goods disappeared behind the fabric.

Luke broke his stare as Nash tightened the drawstring around his waist. Once he finished, he grabbed the tail of his shirt, pulled it over his head, and tossed it on top of his shorts before turning to Luke.

"It's a little loose. What do you think?"

Nash twisted first this way and then the other, eventually turning his butt toward Luke. The shorts were too big for Nash; even cinched up they barely hung from his slender butt. Luke licked his lips at the ivory white skin coming out of the suit and the tiny tangle of blond hair nestled at the top of his ass. The sight of the additional piercings through his nipples excited Luke more than he expected. He was glad he'd worn compression shorts under his trunks. It helped hide his growing reaction to Nash, which would resemble a personal pup tent over his crotch.

Luke swallowed hard. "They're a little big, I guess. But they'll work."

Nash jiggled again and they slipped lower on his butt until Luke could only wonder what kept them up. He looked at Luke with a grin. "You sure they're okay? Seems like they might fall off."

"Nah, they're great." Luke licked his lips. "Yeah, great."

NASH'S STOMACH knotted as he stared at Luke while waiting to see what he was going to do. The teasing banter they'd been exchanging made him hope they were becoming more comfortable with each other, but now Luke had been stalling on the bank of the lake for at least fifteen minutes. One thing after another kept him from getting into the water. Nash paddled closer, wondering what was going on.

"Luke, come on. It feels great."

"Yeah, okay. Give me a sec." He fiddled with the hem of his T-shirt, pulling it up and letting it drop, unconsciously giving a better tease show than some of the strippers in Atlanta. The glimpse of Luke's flat stomach was having its effect. Nash moved closer until he sat on a submerged rock a few feet from Luke.

"What's up? I thought everything was okay."

Luke pressed his hands down his torso and shrugged, his eyes never meeting Nash's. "Yeah. It's all good. But, yeah…."

"What? It can't be that big of a deal."

"I'm kinda hairy," Luke blurted out.

"So?"

"Yeah, well. Some people don't like hairy guys. I tried keeping it shaved but it itches like crazy." His gaze dropped. "Besides, who would see it?"

Nash stood and made his way up the rocky shoreline to Luke, grabbed his shirt, and pulled it over his head with no further ceremony. He tossed the shirt onto the grass and stood admiring Luke's chest.

"Your fur is fucking hot. Don't let anyone tell you otherwise. Now stop being a dipshit." With a light slap on Luke's stomach, Nash walked back into the lake, submerging to his neck. The sight of Luke without a shirt sent pulses of attraction through Nash. He hoped the cool water would help bring his cock down from the raging erection it was. But instead he only got harder as he watched Luke climb into the water.

So far as Nash was concerned, Luke's chest was about as perfect as possible. The dusting of hair across his pecs darkened to a line down his stomach, which disappeared into the cutoff jeans he wore. His broad shoulders tapered to a waist that had a thick Adonis belt coming from both sides. Whoever had Luke worried that he didn't look hot was a twisted son of a bitch.

Luke started into the water, following Nash. When he reached knee deep, he stepped off a rock shelf and instantly submerged to midchest. Nash chuckled at his gasp.

"Man! It's kinda cold."

"Nah, you're being a pussy. Or are you worried about shrinkage?"

Luke snorted and splashed Nash. "Not me. Shrinkage isn't a problem."

Nash shot a rooster tail of water at Luke and drenched him.

"You fucker! I'm gonna get your ass." Luke launched himself at Nash while the taller man took off swimming. But Luke was a strong swimmer and caught him in a few strokes. He grabbed Nash's shoulders and shoved him under.

Nash came up sputtering and flipped his head to get the wet hair off his face. "Oh, you want to play that way."

He grabbed as Luke yelped and dodged. They dove and wrestled until they both gasped for air. They'd moved farther into the lake until the water was over Luke's head. To keep from being pushed under again, he wrapped his legs around Nash. But now, with his crotch pressed against Nash's stomach, Luke's erection was obvious. Their gazes met. Luke blushed and released the leg lock. "Sorry, didn't—"

Nash wrapped his arms around Luke and pulled him tight. The kiss he planted went on for several minutes and left them both winded.

"Stop apologizing. You're not doing anything I'm not enjoying," Nash said.

Muscular legs wrapped around Nash's midsection, and in an instant, they were tight against each other. Luke slipped his work-toughened fingers through Nash's wet hair and pulled them into a snug embrace. Their lips met again. A slow kiss this time, but the fire it ignited in Nash was like nothing he'd felt before. As the kiss faded away, Luke nibbled at his ear and soon had Nash moaning in response.

Luke released his leg lock, but it seemed to be a reluctant gesture. "I think we better stop while we can."

Rock-hard and throbbing, Nash's cock drove his desired response more than his brain. But slowly Luke's words sunk in and he realized they were in a public lake and making out like a couple of horny teenagers. This trip was supposed to be a visit with a friend, not the two of them screwing like rabbits at the first opportunity. He leaned in and gave Luke a soft kiss.

"You're probably right. 'Cause I know I'm thinking with the little head right now."

Luke chuckled and nodded in agreement. "Yeah, something like that." He swam back a few feet so he could touch bottom. "I brought blow-up rafts. We could float around and relax until we get hungry."

"Sounds good to me. I'll cool off in the water and let you blow—something." Nash treaded water, hoping his hard-on would go down, but seeing Luke's butt as he climbed out of the water wasn't helping.

Luke chuckled as he moved to the pickup and rummaged through the box he'd brought. "They're in here somewhere." He paused and smirked at Nash. "And yes, I'm ignoring your comment."

He paddled closer to the shore so he could watch. Luke glanced toward him. "What?"

"Oh, just admiring the view."

Luke waved him off and focused on the search. "Here they are!" He ran back to the lake holding a wad of plastic in each hand. When he was close, he tossed one to Nash.

"There's yours. But you have to—" He glanced at Nash with a cocked eyebrow. "Blow it up."

"That's fine. I'm good at blowing things." Nash smirked at Luke. "Oh, inflating them too."

Luke stared at him before a grin broke across his face. "If you say so, I'll take your word for it."

"I could show you if you'd like."

"Whatever."

Nash peered over the top of his raft and saw Luke's face had become an interesting shade of pink. He decided teasing Luke was one of his new favorite hobbies.

It didn't take much time to inflate the rafts and soon they were both floating on the calm lake surface. The hot sun felt soothing on Nash's back as the lazy day unwound. The two of them teased and challenged each other, but mostly they spent the afternoon becoming better acquainted.

Nash said, "This is nice. Floating around in the lake. I haven't done this since I was a kid. I can't imagine many things that would be more relaxing."

Luke paddled closer and rested his chin across his folded arms. "You haven't said much about where you grew up. Tell me about your hometown before I go blathering off again."

Nash tensed. "Ozark, Alabama. Backwater of the world. Although it has an army base, which can make things more interesting."

Luke's smile grew wider. "Oh? Hot soldiers to stare at?"

Nash decided he'd shared enough of his life history for now. "What do you use the mule for?" Nash asked to change the subject.

Luke hesitated but answered Nash's question. "He's a jumping mule. I got him in trade from a guy in Arkansas. But I haven't used him much."

"Jumping, like a dressage horse?"

"No. More like hunting raccoons. You follow the dogs riding the mule. When you come to a fence, you put a blanket over it and he jumps it. Then you get back on and ride after the dogs."

"You hunted raccoons?"

"Did some when I was a kid. Don't anymore. But I like Jack and don't have the heart to sell him."

"And the horses?"

Luke turned to Nash, and his expression changed to one of surprise and concern. "Shit. You're burned. We need to get something on you."

Nash slid off into the water, holding onto the raft. "It doesn't feel hot."

"It will. Soon. Let's get you doctored."

They made their way to shore, and Luke tossed him a towel. Once they got back to the tent, Luke dug out the tube of burn cream from the first aid kit and tossed it to Nash.

He carefully slathered his chest and arms with the white ointment. He struggled to reach his back until Luke took the tube. He watched Luke coat his fingers and braced himself for the first touch.

Both hands landed at the same instant and Nash gasped softly. There was no pain from the burn, but the sensations that ran through his body were far too strong to be generated by someone he'd only met in person yesterday. However he tried to explain the attraction, its existence was undeniable. He relaxed and enjoyed the contact. By the time Luke finished, Nash's cock was hard again. *Where are we going with this? Why am I so attracted to this man?* He watched as Luke put everything away.

He shifted his gaze as Luke turned back to him. "You hungry? I could start fixing supper."

Nash let out a sigh. He didn't want to pressure Luke, but the attraction was undeniable. Pulling his emotions into line, he realized he was starved. "Sounds good. I could eat."

Nash gathered their shirts and rafts from the edge of the lake while Luke unloaded wood he'd brought from home. Nash carefully put his shirt on over his cream-slathered back and laid out Luke's tee so it could dry.

"If you'd grab the cooler, I'd appreciate it. I brought the stuff for hot dogs and s'mores."

"Sounds great. What can I do to help?"

"I've got a box of matches in the camping stuff. Would you grab it?"

Luke found a couple of handfuls of twigs and small sticks from around their site and was ready when Nash got back with the matches. He lit one, held it under the pile of twigs, and a few seconds later, a wisp of smoke came from the wood, which was soon followed by an eruption of flame. With a few carefully placed branches, the fire burned in earnest.

Luke turned to Nash. "Won't be long now."

LUKE ATE the last of his hotdog while he watched Nash. The city boy roasted the wiener to within an inch of its life, then covered it with mustard. But he seemed to be enjoying himself.

"They okay?" Luke asked.

Nash licked the mustard from his fingers and grinned. "That was dog number, what, four? I guess I'd forgot how good these things taste when you cook them over a fire."

"They are pretty good." Luke paused. "How long has it been since you've been camping?"

"Not since I've been in Atlanta—no car and less money. It was probably junior high, maybe fifteen years ago."

"I have the stuff to make s'mores if you want."

"Man, that sounds outstanding. You're going to fatten me up. I'll have to live on the treadmill for a week once I get back."

"Don't worry. If you're looking for a workout, you can help me unload a truck of hay tomorrow."

"Really?"

"Yeah, couple hundred bales of alfalfa for the horses. It'll work off all those hotdogs, plus dessert."

"It's a deal! Get out the stuff for s'mores."

In a few minutes, the graham crackers and chocolate bars were ready, and he and Nash concentrated on roasting the marshmallows. Luke's kept bursting into flame followed by frantic blowing to extinguish the blackening torch. Eventually they had marshmallows charred on the outside with molten white cream oozing from the cracks.

Nash slid his marshmallow onto a graham cracker, slipped on the piece of chocolate, and mashed it in place with another cracker. After a few seconds of blowing on it to cool it down, he took the first bite. His eyes almost closed as he chewed, swallowed, and sighed. "Really good!"

Luke crammed his treat together and wolfed it down in a few bites. The soft cream and melting chocolate filled his senses, and he remembered all the happy memories he had of making these childhood treats. Before long they were working on marshmallow number two, which was eaten with more deliberation.

"You want to split one? I don't want a whole one," Luke asked.

"Sure, sounds like a plan."

Luke put together the ingredients while Nash roasted the marshmallow. Only the glowing coals were left by this point, so the marshmallow toasted nicely. Luke trapped the hot chunk of fluff between the crackers and held it out to Nash. "Visitors get first bite."

Nash leaned close, took a bite, and chewed it slowly. He swallowed and turned to Luke with a smile. "They're probably better when they don't look like a piece of charcoal."

Luke took his share and after a minute nodded in agreement. "Yup, less ash definitely makes it taste better." He held it out again and grinned as Nash bit off another piece. Luke swallowed the last bit before leaning forward to run his finger along the corner of Nash's mouth.

"Missed a bit."

"Really? Let me see."

The caution fled as Nash took Luke's hand in his and licked each finger clean. Jolts of pleasure shot through him each time Nash's mouth ran over a digit. With a knowing look, he took Luke's other hand. One finger at a time, Nash sucked off the bits of their dessert.

"There. All clean."

Luke trembled by the time Nash finished. He tried to talk several times but couldn't form words. He stopped to collect himself and managed to squeak out, "It's pretty dark. I guess we should hit the hay."

"Sounds like a good plan to me."

Luke pulled a shovel from the pickup and piled dirt over the fire while Nash grabbed a small bag he'd brought. Luke tossed the shovel back in the vehicle, grabbed the inflated rafts, and threw them into the tent.

He turned and bumped into Nash. Standing with their bodies almost touching, he could smell Nash's subtle scent.

"My bag. In the pickup," Luke stammered.

Nash held up a small backpack. "This it? I thought you might want it so I brought it."

"Yeah, that's the one." He took the bag from Nash and ducked into the tent. Nash followed and zipped the door closed. Luke arranged the rafts and covered them with a sheet.

"I doubt we'll need anything over us. It doesn't cool off that much at night."

Nash unlaced his swimsuit and let it drop to the floor. Luke glanced up in time to see a naked Nash catch his shorts with a toe and toss them into the corner. Their gazes met, and Luke felt like he was about to combust.

"I sleep nude, usually. But I can do something else if it makes you uncomfortable," Nash said.

You mean other than making me want things to go a lot further than a kiss? "No, no problem."

"Good." Nash lowered himself to the bed and sprawled across it. Luke swallowed hard at the sight of this man's pale, almost ghostly, body against the white sheet. He unbuttoned his shorts, let them fall to the floor, and toed them to the opposite side. He knelt on the edge of the bed, unsure of everything. As his nervousness lessened he moved to lie on the mattress with his back to Nash.

Luke started to relax when an arm slipped over him and Nash began tracing patterns across his chest. His breath coming in shudders, Luke asked, "What are you doing?"

"Finishing what we started today. It's dark and we're not in the middle of a public lake anymore."

Luke started a chuckle that became a gasp when Nash scraped a fingernail over his hard nipple. "Oh God, that feels great." He let himself go, his pleasure building with each pass of Nash's hands. But panic built faster and ate at Luke's confidence. He grabbed Nash's wrists and pulled them away.

"What's wrong?"

"I need to tell you something. We need to talk."

"Okay. What do we need to talk about?"

"Me. I might have kinda misled you when we talked online and what I told you yesterday."

Nash pulled his hands back and lifted himself on one elbow. "Okay."

"I kinda made it sound like I'd had dates and done stuff, other than with Bobby. Well, that's not true. I've only done stuff with him, and he is kind of...."

"Kinky?"

"Actually I was thinking more... vanilla."

"You still doing stuff with him?"

"Oh, God no! We're done. I'd never lie about that. But...."

"But you were worried I'd think you were more experienced than you are."

"Yeah, something like that." Luke rubbed his hand through his hair. "I wanted to warn you I might not be very good."

"Do you want to go further than you did with him?"

"Hell, yes. I suggested stuff, like off the web. But he didn't want to do anything different. He said the stuff I found was weird."

"What a delightful prick. Well don't sweat it. I have enough experience for both of us." Nash paused and considered Luke. "Is there anything that really turns you on?"

Luke thought his face was probably glowing in the dark it was so hot, but he managed to get out his answer. "I like feet. I think some guys have sexy feet. I mean all the normal stuff too, but feet are hot."

Nash dropped against Luke again and couldn't help but chuckle. "A little foot fetish from my hot cowboy. I think we can figure out some stuff you'll like. You relax and let's see what happens?"

Luke's doubts crept through him, but his desire for Nash overrode his concern. "Yeah, that sounds good."

Nash slipped his arms around Luke and caressed him again. A line of fire followed each touch until a flame of lust etched its way across Luke's chest. Nash pushed his hand lower and groped Luke through his compression shorts. The throb of his pulse pounded in his ears as Nash wrapped his hand around Luke's trapped cock, slowly squeezing its length until he rubbed the tip of his thumb into the underside of Luke's shaft.

"No, no. Oh, you gotta stop." He grabbed Nash's hand and peeled it away.

Nash kissed the tip of Luke's ear and whispered, "You okay?"

"Oh, yeah. But you had me about ready to pop."

A soft chuckle filled the tent. "Well that's not the worst thing you could've said. But we'll let you calm down."

He turned in Nash's arms and shot him a wolfish grin. "My turn."

Nash caught his face between his hands and tilted him so their eyes met. "I can guarantee you that nothing you found online is going to shock me. So relax and enjoy yourself."

Luke hesitated before lying back. He first touched Nash's face, enjoying the raspy texture under his fingertips. He pressed his nose against the nape of Nash's neck and inhaled deeply, filling his senses with the essence of the man beside him. After kissing down Nash's long, sinuous neck, he flicked his tongue against the prominent Adam's apple.

He found the hard points of flesh created by Nash's erect nipples and discovered a metal ring hanging from each one. He tugged on them as he chewed on the side of Nash's neck, whose groans filled the tent. "Shit. You don't seem so inexperienced."

"I didn't say I haven't looked up stuff."

The tent filled with the scent of sweat and the musk of two horny men. Luke slipped his fingers through the patch of hair surrounding Nash's cock and traced the thick blue vein running its length. Clear liquid coated his finger as he rubbed over the tip of Nash's dick. As he lowered his lips closer, Nash gently gripped his shoulders.

"We need to play safe, and the porn you've been watching isn't a good example." Nash found his bag, flicked on a flashlight, and rummaged inside. It didn't take long before he pulled out a handful of condom packets and a small bottle of lube.

Spreading them on the bed, he grinned at Luke. "The ones in the red packets are cherry flavored. The others are plain. The lube is safe with either. But trust me, you don't want a mouth full of dick covered in spermicide. That shit's nasty."

Luke considered Nash's instructions before staring at the condoms he held. "I'm not sure…."

"I just grabbed a handful. It's not like we're going to need all these. You know, the whole be prepared thing. But if you want to go down on me… here." Nash handed Luke one of the flavored condoms and lay back.

Luke fumbled in the dark tent but got the package open and unrolled onto Nash's shaft. As he stroked the hard cock, he planted more small kisses down Nash's torso. The combination of hard and soft along with his rich scent made Luke want to go a lot further than anything he'd done with Bobby. He wasn't certain he was ready to talk about some of the things he wanted to try, though.

He reached Nash's cock and slipped the head in his mouth. He couldn't resist flicking his tongue against the metal piercing, which was making him want more. The pulsing head felt good as Luke pressed farther, wanting to get the whole length in his mouth. Nash's cock wedged against the back of his throat, but Luke couldn't take it anymore. As he pulled off, Nash made soft squeaking sounds. He raised his head until only the crown was in his mouth and slipped his tongue along the edge several times.

Nash curled to his side and groped Luke through the shorts. He moaned around Nash's cock as the pressure built again. He let the shaft slip from his lips and lay back to enjoy what Nash was doing. The night air hit his newly exposed skin as Nash pulled Luke's shorts down to his ankles and then off.

When his cock snapped free, Nash whistled softly. "Nice."

"Really? Bobby always said it was too big. He wouldn't ever do anything but a hand job."

"Bobby Joe Dipshit is an idiot. This'll be fun."

He fished through the small pile of condoms and pulled out one in a gold packet. He held it in front of Luke and waved it back and forth as he smirked. "We don't want one that's too small."

Luke flashed hot as Nash tore open the packet and unrolled the Magnum condom down Luke's length. The simple touch drove Luke to the edge. "Easy. I'm close."

"Me too. Let's relax a little."

Nash kissed the tip of Luke's cock and then moved until they were lip to lip again. "Let's ease into this. I love how sexy your lips are. I'd like to kiss you for a really long time."

A lump formed in Luke's throat at the thought someone wanted to make love with him and not just get off. He realized he'd never answered Nash; swallowing quickly, he nodded. "Yeah. I'd like that."

Nash's masculine scent intertwined with the faint smell of smoke and the sound of water lapping gently against the shore. It curled through his system, and any remaining concerns about going too fast melted in a whirlwind of desire. His lips parted and their mouths touched. The heat from Nash's kiss wound through his body, and he lost awareness of anything other than Nash and his scalding touch.

Their kiss lasted for several long, delicious minutes, escalating Luke's growing lust. Their tongues struggled with each other and Luke became more aggressive. With only a few moves, Nash was pinned beneath him as their crotches ground against each other. His desire grew like nothing he'd experienced before.

Despite his flippant response to Nash's comment about his experience, he worried how well he was doing and how to take the next step. He didn't want this to end with them both just covered with white stuff. He wanted to make love. He wanted to be inside Nash. He wanted to experience the level of intimacy he'd never tried before. Bobby never would let him. But Nash seemed open to anything. Luke moved more urgently, searching for Nash's opening as his desires overwhelmed his thoughts.

As he struggled, Nash wrapped his legs around Luke's waist and caressed his face. "It's okay, Luke. I want it too. Just move me where you want. And relax. I guarantee it will be good."

"But...."

Nash grinned as he curled to Luke and teasingly grabbed his nipples. "Relax. I'm as ready for this as you are. It's been a while since I've been with someone. And I'd like to do this with you."

Luke struggled again, trying to find Nash's sweet spot. After a few minutes the whole situation became more frustrating than sexy and was taking its toll on Luke. Nash grabbed his knees and pulled them higher. Luke pressed forward, and this time he met with success. He ran his dick up and down Nash's cleft, the heat and need

46

filling him again. He pressed harder with each pass, wanting to bury himself inside.

"Luke...."

He froze in place, unsure of what had gone wrong. "What?"

"Relax. Everything's going fine. I think we'd both have more fun if you got me a little more ready."

Luke filled with confusion before realizing what he had almost done. "Oh crap. I'm so sorry. I could have hurt you if—"

Nash cut him off with a wave of his hand. "It's okay. Like I said, I have enough experience for both of us. Do you have the lube?"

Luke scrambled around and found the small bottle. With a feeling of triumph, he held it up. "Yeah, I found it!"

A soft chuckle drifted to Luke's ears. "Be generous. I'm sure we can use one of your monster camo towels to clean up afterwards."

Luke nodded and snapped open the cap. He squirted a thin stream on Nash and then slipped the tip of his finger over the soaked opening. It pressed in easily, and he was glad to hear a soft moan.

"Oh, that's it. Deeper. Aww," Nash said.

Luke sank inside, enjoying the tight heat. He pressed his hand against Nash's buttcheek and paused. Slowly he slipped almost out before sinking his fingers back inside until his knuckles pressed against Nash. He could hear the gasps of pleasure as he buried his fingers deeper.

Panting with excitement, Luke let his fingers slip out and added more lube to them both. Focused on Nash, he added another finger and slowly stretched him even more. Time seemed to freeze as he lost himself in exploring his partner.

"That's it. You're doing so good. I'm ready, Luke."

He glanced up, his cock steel hard in excitement. "You sure you—"

"Oh, hell yes. Do it. I'm ready for more than a few fingers."

"You sure? 'Cause I'm—"

Nash arched his back, dug his heels into Luke's muscular thighs, and pulled them together. "Stop talking and start fucking!"

Luke coated his shaft with lube and pressed forward. Fire shot through him as he slipped inside Nash. The tight heat drove Luke to the edge. Pausing, he leaned against Nash and fought for control. He shuddered when Nash ran his hands over him.

"No. No, no, no. I'm so close."

Nash practically growled his response. "Keep that up and you might be able to manage something only a few people have."

Trickles of lightning rippled through Luke, and pressing forward, he buried himself inside Nash. He throbbed with excitement as he pinned Nash beneath him and ground their bodies against each other. His gentle exploration gave way to heightened passion. His thrusts came fast and hard. Loud groans of delight from Nash drove him to new levels.

Nash thrashed and whimpered under him, seeming to enjoy the hard pounding he was getting. Luke sped toward the top of his building climax, no longer in control of his body's reaction. Before he dove into ecstasy, Nash locked his muscles, clamping down on Luke in midthrust.

"Holy fuck!" Nash screamed.

Nash tensed further and convulsed as his muscles gripped Luke's length. Shoved over the edge, Luke began to fill the condom. Nash's movements lessened, but Luke pounded Nash as his climax peaked.

Sounding like two animals in rut, the men were in the pleasure throes for what seemed an eternity. Luke let out a final drawn-out groan as the last convulsion rolled through his body and left him feeling like a limp washcloth. With a contented sigh, he lowered himself on top of Nash.

"That was so good," Luke said.

Nash traced through the short hair covering Luke's head. The caress felt strong and demanding, exactly what Luke wanted. He'd enjoyed being in charge this time, but he was ready to change roles too. He ran the tips of his fingers over the stubble on Nash's face. The dark shadow of hair left no doubt that he was with a man.

"That was amazing. And you were nervous about how you would do. Let me tell you, that was mind-blowing sex," Nash said.

Luke chuckled and dropped his face to snuggle against Nash. He kissed Nash's ear and whispered, "It was amazing, but I'm pooped. Apparently I need to be back in top wrestling form for hot monkey sex."

Nash laughed in response. "I'm exhausted too. That's enough for tonight. But give me a few hours and I'll be up for monkey sex as often as we can work it in."

Luke pulled Nash in for another kiss. They held each other and let the soft breeze dry their sweaty bodies and the rustling sounds of life all around them ease them back from their euphoria. Nash leaned in and whispered, "Actually I lied."

Luke cautiously studied Nash. "About what?"

"I told you it took a lot to get me to come from being fucked...."

"Yeah?"

"Actually, it's never happened before. I've faked it before with a few people, but you're the first to actually make it happen."

"Really?" Luke asked.

"Oh yeah, I've been close before, but you were hitting my sweet spot in ways no one else ever has."

Luke kissed the side of Nash's neck, flicking his tongue to taste a bit of salty sweat. "Good." He moved to sit up and felt a tug. The scent that drifted into his nostrils gave him an answer that set Luke to chuckling. He planted another peck on Nash's chin.

"I think we might want another dip in the lake. We seem to have managed to glue ourselves together."

NASH WAS in a great mood as the pickup climbed out of their hidden camping spot. He let his arm drape over the open window, enjoying the cool morning breeze as the sound of the rumbling engine almost masked the crunch of leaf and stone. Last night really had been amazing. He hadn't lied to Luke. That never happened before. With most of his tricks, he not only couldn't get off from being fucked, it was work to get off at all. Too many of them were repellent, so far as Nash was concerned, and some were dangerous. That had been proven with the one who'd put him in the hospital.

"You're awfully quiet over there."

"Just reliving last night. Over and over again. Damn, you were amazing. I can't believe you were worried."

"I'd never done it before, and I'm sure you've been with more guys than I have."

Nash turned to stare out the window. "Yeah, that's a pretty safe bet."

"But you still enjoyed yourself? It was by far the best sex I've ever had."

Nash grinned at Luke. "It was good. Bobby Dipshit is not only an idiot, but a terrible lover."

Luke started laughing, and Nash couldn't help but think this was the most relaxed he'd seen the man. A smile traveled across Nash's face. He was pretty relaxed after yesterday too, and a tingle in his ass let him know how much fun he'd had.

He turned back to Luke. "Seriously. Bobby must be pretty bad."

"Well, compared to last night he's terrible. But then he always said butt fucking was gross." Panic formed on his face as he glanced to Nash. "Sorry. That's what he called it."

Nash waved the comment aside. "Don't sweat it." He rode quietly as he considered the man he'd only met face-to-face a few days ago. As he contemplated his companion, Nash still couldn't shake the feeling that Luke's ex was somehow familiar.

Nash was thrown forward and missed cracking his skull on the windshield by a fraction of an inch. By the time he got his bearings, a character straight out of *Deliverance* stalked around the pickup toward Luke. His stomach knotted. The man was carrying a shotgun.

Luke started yelling before he got the window down. "Koslov! Are you crazy? I almost hit you."

Nash could see the wild look in the man's eyes from where he sat. That and the way he brandished the gun made Nash think he was crazy enough to use the weapon.

"Those animals of yours. I'm going to kill them, Meyers. I've told you to keep them off my property."

"Koslov, I check every time you say they are out, and it's never my cattle. What did you see this time?"

"No, these were yours. Cows with humps on their backs. I know what I saw."

"Okay, I'll check as soon as we get home."

Nash drew back when the man waved the gun at Luke. "I'm killing them. I'll shoot them all. Next time they're on my property. It's within my rights."

Luke pushed the gun barrel upward and stepped out of the pickup. "Now, Koslov. You need to watch where you point that thing. It might accidentally go off and shoot someone. I'm sure whatever is on your property isn't my cattle. But I'll double-check. Besides, I don't have brahmas, so if they have humps, they aren't mine."

"God dammit! I'll kill them! I have my rights. I own my land and I'll fight for it."

Luke pushed the gun away again when it swung upward, this time more forcefully. "No one's trying to take your land. Are you sure it wasn't the elk again?"

"No! It wasn't the goddamn elk. It was your cows."

Nash recognized the signs of someone whose connection with reality was pretty tenuous. Luke seemed to be handling the man fine, but Nash had dealt with hysterically unreasonable people before. He thought having someone standing close to back Luke up would be a good idea. He pulled the door handle, and the crazy man swung his gun and pointed it at Nash.

"Is this one of the Feds you brought? Thought you'd get me with double talk? I'll shoot anyone who comes on my property. I have the right to bear arms. It's right there in the Constitution."

Nash froze in place, uncertain what to do next.

Luke stepped in and grabbed the gun, ejected the shells into the dirt, and handed it back. "You can keep your damn gun. But you can't point it at my friends. I'll check on the cattle as soon as I can. But you're going to end up in jail if you aren't careful."

"I have a right—"

"I'm going home now. I'll check my stock. You need to cool off."

The man's face was crimson, and he was still waving the gun and screaming about his rights as they drove away. Nash watched him until he was certain they were out of range.

"He's not as bad as he seems. Ian moved here about ten years ago from somewhere on the West Coast. As people around here say, he's a bit touched."

"He's a crazy motherfucker is what he is. It's a miracle you didn't get shot."

"Yeah, he's gotten a little out of hand. His episodes have never been this bad before. I bet it's an elk from the refuge again. That's what it was the last few times. He'd get in less trouble over shooting my cows than one of the elk."

"He seems like one of those crazy survivalists."

Luke shrugged. "Lots of people around here have guns, and there is still an attitude that we take care of our own problems. But Koslov goes too far."

"Like I said, he's a crazy motherfucker. That's what he is."

The next few miles were quiet, but as they pulled into Luke's driveway, his phone rang.

"Luke Meyers speaking." Luke listened for a minute before he replied, "Uh-huh. Tomorrow, then?"

After another long pause, he responded. "I'd rather have it earlier but if that's the best you can do…."

Nash could see from the tightening of Luke's jaw the conversation wasn't going how he wanted. "Okay, see you then."

Luke stared at his phone before turning to Nash. "That was the guy who was supposed to deliver the alfalfa today. He's got truck trouble so it'll be tomorrow. That means the only thing I need to do today is check the cattle to make sure crazy Koslov wasn't right. So I was wondering…."

"What? I'm probably up for it."

"When's the last time you went to a county fair?"

CHAPTER FIVE

IN THE gray of early twilight, Nash enjoyed watching the people moving like a strongly choreographed dance down the aisles of food carts, games, and strange contraptions no one should be without. Surveying the people milling around him and Luke, he wouldn't have thought this many even lived in this county. It had been a long time since Nash was at a fair. Back sometime when he was a kid in 4-H he'd guess. Nash chuckled. Showing those damn pigs. Squealing, oinking, very smart pigs.

"Hey, what do you want to do first?"

"I'm getting hungry. How about you?"

"Sounds like a plan. How do you feel about corn dogs?"

"You mean your favorite fast food?"

"Oh, yeah. We covered this. But I swear, none of them tastes like the ones from the fair. I've tried all the frozen junk, and they don't measure up."

"You're a corn dog connoisseur, I guess."

Luke chuckled and nodded toward one of the food vendors. "That one's pretty good. I've had their dogs before."

They moved to the back of the line and Nash watched them spear each wiener with a sharp stick, coat them with cornbread batter, and then slip it into hot oil. The smell coming through the screened windows was having its effect on Nash. He was salivating and his stomach growling by the time they reached the order window.

"Whatcha need?"

"Two corn dogs." Luke glanced back at Nash and grinned. "Make that four and two limeades."

Nash stepped up with his wallet in his hand. Luke pushed his money back to him. "My treat. You're my guest."

"I told you that you didn't have to buy my meals for me."

53

Luke waved his hand as he slid a few bills through the window. "Nope, I'm being a good host. A good host doesn't let his guest pay for anything."

"Oh really?"

"Yup, it might even be an Oklahoma law."

"Guess I can't argue with you, then."

About then the vendor slid their meal through the window, and Luke passed one of the plates to Nash. They moved to the condiment station, and Nash made soft gagging noises at the sight of the pile of mustard and ketchup Luke had on his plate.

"What?"

"That's still some nasty shit."

"Oh, it's good. You probably don't dip them in anything."

Nash squirted mustard onto his plate, ran one of the dogs through it, and took a bite. He said around his food, "Mustard only."

They found an unoccupied picnic table to eat at and enjoyed their meal. The food disappeared quickly, and they were soon going through the exhibits again.

"Anything you'd like to see?" Luke asked.

"Can we go check out the animals?"

"Sure! That's usually where I head first. But I figured you'd think that was boring."

Luke threaded them through the crowd and into the first barn. Nash enjoyed walking through the immaculately groomed animals, first moving through row after row of cattle before petting the friendlier horses in their stalls. After walking past a few pens of sheep and goats, they moved into the final building, and deafening noise met them. Nash found himself in a world that took him back to his childhood. He stood still and surveyed the scene: wall-to-wall pigs. He could barely hear for the squeals echoing through the enclosure.

"They're pretty loud. We can duck out if you want."

"Actually, I love pigs. We had them when I was a kid. Not a lot, but my parents raised them to make extra money, and they always had one butchered for us to eat."

"Really? I thought you were raised in town. I guess I've looked pretty stupid telling you stuff you already knew."

Nash turned to Luke and gave him a playful punch on the shoulder. "I only know a little about pigs. Probably half of what I know is wrong. I was in grade school. You've been really good about explaining everything. Relax, I'm enjoying myself."

Luke looked dubious. "If you say so, but why didn't you tell me you grew up on a farm?"

Memories he didn't want to deal with flooded back and filled him. Nash knew he tensed, but he couldn't stop himself. "Let's just say the pigs were one of the few good memories from that time in my life and leave it at that."

Luke studied him and nodded. They worked their way through the barn, which rang with grunts and high-pitched squeals. A few animals ran to the fence as they walked past, and Nash scratched through their coarse hair. He couldn't resist laughing at one whose water nipple wasn't working the way he wanted, so he banged it until it did and started drinking.

They wandered out of the animal barns, and he waited while Luke glanced around. He turned to Nash. "Okay, so we can go through the 4-H buildings or hit the midway."

"Midway, definitely. I've behaved long enough. I want to ride stuff until I barf."

"Tilt-A-Whirl here we come!"

A few minutes later found them at the end of a long line for one of the more popular rides. Nash was surprised to see such a variety of people. It didn't look much different from some of the areas in Atlanta. Same designer clothes for most of the high school kids, even a few sporting the latest haircuts. The younger kids with their parents were classic Americana. There might have been a few more country boys wearing baseball caps advertising the local feed mill, but they were hot too. It saddened him to think this crowd would probably be offended, and maybe violent, if he were kissing Luke the way some of the young guys kissed the girls with them.

"You okay? You seem deep in thought," Luke said.

Nash gave him a strained smile. "Yeah, I'm great. Hey, after this ride let's grab some more food. I'm hungry."

Luke shrugged. "Sounds good to me. But don't expect me to hold your hair back when you barf."

THEY MADE their way out the big double garage door at the end of the building, and the evening breeze washed across Luke's skin as the calls and other sounds of the midway surrounded them. He couldn't help but keep glancing at Nash as he zeroed in on a new vendor. He smiled as the tall young man continued to surprise him. *He likes pigs? Who likes pigs?* But he was coming to realize he didn't know much about Nash.

"What do ya need, buddy?"

Luke glanced at the menu and turned to the vendor. "Just a funnel cake. With lots of powdered sugar. Oh, and a Dr Pepper."

He paid for his purchase and returned carrying a piping hot, fresh-made funnel cake to a waiting Nash. He sat the overflowing paper plate between them.

"Careful. They made it while I was standing there so it's really hot."

Nash broke off a piece, passing it from one hand to the other until he thought it had cooled enough and bit into the fried dough. Luke laughed at the contortions Nash was going through trying to swallow the hot treat. Once he got it down, he grabbed the pop and chugged it.

By this time Luke was laughing hysterically. "I told you it was hot."

Nash drained the Dr Pepper before stopping for air. "But you didn't tell me the fucker was brown lava!"

Still laughing, Luke choked out a reply. "Sugar-covered brown lava."

Nash stared at him, then grinned. "Asshole."

"I got one of those, yup." Luke pulled off a bite of funnel cake and ate it.

Nash reached over, pulled off a second piece for himself, and carefully bit into it. This time there was no squeal of pain. "Okay, it's pretty good."

"See. Stick with me and I'll show you the good stuff."

"You mean fried, fried, and fried?"

"Maybe."

They soon had the dessert reduced to a single bite. Nash picked up the morsel and took a nip from one side. Then he reached across the table and fed the rest to Luke. As the bite of food slipped into his mouth, Luke filled with an emotion he refused to categorize.

As Nash drew his hand back, Luke grabbed it and pulled him close. He narrowed the distance, sucked Nash's finger in his mouth, and cleaned it of the sugar stuck to it.

"Well ain't this sweet. The fairy found another one of his kind."

Anger and frustration flooded Luke's system. This wasn't the way he'd hoped the evening would go. He could hear the grunts of assent from several mouths. *Great. The thugs I went to high school with.*

Luke turned to the men and glared. "David, why don't you scurry back under your rock and take your buddies with you." He turned and locked eyes with the man leering at them. Nash pulled his hand away, looking like he was ready to run. Luke set his jaw as any fear evaporated under the flood of anger. *Why can't they leave me alone?*

"Looks like you found you a little woman. Or are you the pussy?"

Fury burned through Luke as he stood and glared at the big man who'd ruined his evening. "You want me to whip your ass right here in front of your buddies? 'Cause that's what you're shooting for."

"You little fart. You think you're such hot shit. I should stomp your face." He shifted his glare to Nash. "And your girlfriend too. We'll fix both of you."

Luke sensed Nash's movement and figured he was about to make a dash for safety. He was surprised when he glanced over and Nash stood at his shoulder with his arms crossed, glaring at David and his friends. Luke felt something he hadn't before when Nash rested his hand on his shoulder. His support made this whole incident even more infuriating. He glared at David and stepped forward.

"Get your ass outta my face, Walker. We weren't doing anything to you."

David lunged, caught Luke, and tried to shove him backward. Luke used the momentum to roll him into a chokehold and clamp it on tight.

"All right, that's enough. Let him go, Luke."

Luke soured even further at the familiar voice and uniform. He slowly released his hold and David twisted away, rubbing his throat.

"He jumped us. We weren't doing nothing and he jumped us."

"Oh, shut up, David. I know you were causing trouble. Y'all get outta here. I don't want to see you again tonight."

David backed up another step before turning to his friends—at least, the ones who hadn't disappeared into the midway when the cop appeared. Tension filled Luke as he tried to control his anger. "You know we didn't do anything. We were enjoying the fair."

"You can't rub it in people's faces, Luke."

"We didn't rub anything in anyone's face. We were just having a night out."

"I've been watching you. You might be able to be all over each other in San Francisco or wherever your friend is from, but not in Stillwell."

The anger seethed just below the surface for Luke. This wasn't a lecture he wanted to hear again. "Al, we didn't do anything illegal. Actually, David and his asshole friends threatened us. You know it wasn't our fault."

The officer smiled and shrugged. "Didn't say you were doing a thing wrong. Just some friendly advice. You know how folks around here feel about homosexuals. You should be careful."

The cop turned and melted back into the crowd. Luke glared at his back until it disappeared, trying to keep his anger from erupting.

"What an asshole."

Luke's jaw clenched and he nodded in agreement. "Yeah, asshole would be the nicest thing I can think of." Luke sighed as the anger soured in his stomach. "I think I'm ready to leave. I've had about all the small-town fun I can handle for one night."

CHAPTER SIX

NASH WOKE to the clatter of pans. The house had been fairly warm when they got back from the fair last night, so Luke turned on the air conditioner. As a result, Nash pulled a sheet and blanket over himself during the night, but more importantly it meant he wasn't hearing the collection of morning sounds he'd gotten yesterday, and he missed them.

He stretched and kicked the covers onto the floor. After climbing from the bed, he moved to the window and stared out. The tranquility of the whole scene crept into his system until the relaxed state felt natural. This was nothing like real life. That he was waking up at a time when he normally would have been going to sleep was proof of that.

There was a loud bang, followed by a few choice words from the other end of the house. Nash chuckled and started out the door before he remembered he was naked. He grabbed a pair of shorts from his bag and pulled them on as he made his way down the hallway. He rounded the corner to find Luke on his hands and knees wiping something from the floor.

"Just the way I like my men, on their knees."

"Oh, fuck you. I dropped the whole bowl of pancake batter on the floor."

"You can make pancakes?"

"I was going to give it a shot."

"Where'd you get the recipe?"

"Looked on Google."

Nash chuckled and jumped onto the counter, tucking his feet under him as Luke cleaned the floor. Luke was only wearing a pair of athletic shorts, and right now they were stretched tight across his ass. Nash settled in to enjoy the show. Luke made a final swipe with a towel before tossing it into the sink.

"Okay, I guess I'll give this another shot."

Nash jumped off the counter and padded over to help. As he stood there, he realized Luke's scent was having its effect on him. "Damn, you smell fine this morning."

Luke glanced at him, his mouth puckered. "Sorry. I didn't shower yet. I probably stink."

"No, I'm not shitting you. You're making me horny." He ground himself against Luke, enjoying his hardening cock sliding across the inside of his shorts.

Luke pushed back but frowned. "Knock it off. I'm trying to make us some breakfast." He nodded at the tent Nash's cock was making. "That doesn't help me focus."

Nash chuckled and moved so he could see the recipe. He grabbed ingredients from the fridge, and working together, they had another bowl of pancake batter made in no time. Nash leaned against the counter as Luke swirled melted butter in the skillet before spooning in small pools of batter.

After a few seconds, the room filled with the aroma of breakfast. Nash watched intently. "They're bubbling. You can flip them now."

Luke scooted the spatula under one of them and flipped it. But in the process, he also managed to sling a trail of batter across the stovetop. "Dang it!"

Nash chuckled and wet a cloth at the sink. He wiped up the spilled liquid as Luke flipped the other cakes, with more success.

"Plates?"

Luke nodded to a corner cabinet. "In there."

Nash grabbed a couple of plates and lined them up beside Luke. A minute or so later, Luke slid the first results of his work onto them. He sat the skillet back on the fire and handed Nash the cakes. "Go ahead and eat them while they're hot. I'll have the next batch."

"Nah, that's okay. I'll butter them and wait for you so we can eat together."

Having gained a little experience, Luke had more success with the next batch. Nash knew Luke was nervous about the meal he'd made for them. But he couldn't resist a little gentle teasing about one of the items he'd set out. He lifted the bottle of corn syrup and grinned at Luke. "Karo syrup?"

Luke shrugged and ducked his head a little. "That's what my granddad always had on his, so I had to have the same. I have maple syrup if you want it. I didn't think about it."

"Nope, this is fine. You should try new things, right?"

Luke grinned as Nash coated his pancakes with clear syrup. He cut a bite off and slipped it between his lips. A flood of sugar filled his mouth, but it wasn't bad. Just different. "Pretty good. I'm going to have a sugar rush by the time I finish this, though."

Luke poured syrup over his pancakes. "That's good, because the hay is coming this afternoon, and I thought we'd ride the fences this morning to make sure none of my cattle are on Koslov's land."

Nash chewed slower and slower, pausing before he swallowed. "Luke, I've never rode a horse. I don't know how to steer them or anything."

"Don't sweat it. You can have Lucy. She's easy to ride."

Apprehension built in Nash as they ate. He was actually terrified of riding the big animals. He'd heard stories about them kicking and biting their owners. What if they stepped on him? They'd break his foot.

"Stop worrying about it. I promise nothing will happen."

Neither man said anything further through the meal. Nash finished the last bite, feeling a buzz from the sugar, and caught Luke's gaze. "Okay, let's get this shit going. When I fall off and the horse stomps me, you're going to take care of me for the rest of my life."

"That's not gonna happen. Come on."

Leaving the dishes piled for later, they walked across the gravel parking area to the corral. There were several horses and the mule, and they were all watching them closely. They opened the gate and stepped through. Nash kept an eye on the animals as Luke latched the gate shut and got two bridles looped over his arm. He handed one of them to Nash. "Hang on to this for a sec."

He walked into the corral, and the horses' tails shot up in the air as they trotted away from him. It took several minutes, but he caught one and slipped the bridle onto its head. He tied it to one of the rings embedded in the corral and eased himself toward the horses again. This time they seemed even more determined to avoid Luke. After they went around the corral a half-dozen times, Nash wondered if this was an even worse idea than he'd originally thought.

As Luke started around again, Nash realized the mule had never moved to join the horses and in fact had stood by him the whole time. He reached out and scratched the animal's neck. "You seem a lot less dangerous than those crazy horses."

One of the horses squealed and kicked backward at Luke. Nash had seen about enough of Luke's calm horses. "Hey, can I ride the mule? He seems chill."

Luke slowed to a stop, then walked back to Nash. He looked at him and the mule before shrugging. "Jack's… different. Sort of has a mind of his own. But if you want to ride him, that's fine with me."

"Will he buck me off or something? I'm not really into a redneck version of hazing."

"No, I wouldn't do that to you. He's never bucked with me. But he does make his opinion known."

"He seems a lot calmer than the horses."

Luke scratched his head and studied the two of them. "He does seem to like you. I haven't ridden him in a while. Let me grab his stuff."

He disappeared into the barn and returned with a different kind of bridle in one hand and a saddle in the other. He tossed the saddle over a horizontal beam that seemed to be there for that purpose and walked to the mule. He scratched the animal behind the ears and slipped the bridle on his head with no trouble. The mule bit down and wiggled the bit in his mouth until he seemed happy with it, then watched as Luke carried the saddle over. He tossed the blanket on and settled it into place. The saddle followed, with Nash focused on each step. Eventually Luke tightened the last cinch and stepped back.

"I think you're good. You might lead him around while I get Maggie saddled."

Needing an outlet for his own nervous energy, he was happy to walk the huge animal he'd soon be riding. He'd only made a few trips around the pen when Luke called to him. "I'm ready. Let's get going before the truck shows up."

Nash followed Luke out and waited while Luke closed the gate, caught his boot in the stirrup, and gracefully seated himself in the saddle. He gave Nash a small grin. "You can use the log to get in the saddle, if you need help."

Nash lifted an eyebrow and walked to Jack's side. Mimicking Luke's motion as best he could, he managed to haul himself into the saddle. He struggled for a second or two getting his right foot into the stirrup. But he managed and then looked over to find Luke watching him with a satisfied expression.

"It shouldn't take long. We could have walked the whole thing. But the horses haven't been out in a few days." He smiled at Nash and his mount. "And Jack too."

The next few minutes were spent threading their way through the small cattle pens close to the house until they were in one of the large pastures. Jack seemed content to follow a few feet behind Luke, and Nash unwound. He particularly enjoyed the sight of Luke's butt flexing with each step. Then he realized he had no idea what they were looking for.

"Hey, Luke. What are we trying to find?"

Luke twisted in the saddle so they were facing each other. "Places where the fence is down. It's possible. Granddad put it in about fifty years ago. But I check it pretty often, especially the side that joins with Koslov's."

The rest of the morning was a slow, relaxing ride. Luke pointed out several features in the landscape Nash would have missed otherwise, but mostly they rode in silence. By the time they returned to the house, it was getting hot and Nash was sore.

They stopped at the gate and Luke dismounted with the same fluid grace. Nash tried to follow suit but discovered his legs didn't work right anymore.

"Need some help?" Luke asked.

"No, I got this," Nash said, too stubborn to admit he needed help. He managed to kick a foot loose and slithered down the mule's side. His foot touched the ground and an instant later he grabbed frantically at the saddle to keep from collapsing.

"Hang on so you don't fall, and try to move your feet a little."

Nash glanced over to see Luke standing close. He first thought Luke was making fun of the fact that he was so sore, but realized that wasn't the case.

"It hurts like a motherfucker."

"Sorry. I didn't think you'd be so sore. It's my fault."

"Oh, bullshit. I'm an adult, and you didn't make me go riding. Besides, I think it's getting better." Nash took a few steps, his teeth clenched against the pain.

"Let's get you some place to sit down. I'll unsaddle and brush out the animals."

"Oh no. I might not be able to carry his saddle over this time, but I'll brush Jack. I owe him that much."

"You sure? You've gotta be pretty saddle sore. I bet the embroidery on your back pockets is permanently branded into your ass."

"Probably so. But I'm still going to groom him."

"All right, if you want." Luke unsaddled the mule and brought Nash a huge brush. He started out tentatively but realized the mule leaned into each stroke and began giving him a thorough brushing. In the process, he managed to work most of the stiffness from his legs. He followed Luke as they led both animals into their pasture and released them. They stood watching the pair graze and Luke turned to him. "I don't know about you, but I'm starved. I've got sandwich stuff and chips."

"Sounds great."

A HOT gust of dust and bits of hay swirled around them as Nash and Luke stood in the open barn door and waved as the semitruck pulled out of the driveway. After it disappeared behind the grove of trees, they focused on getting the last of the hay inside. Luke sank his hay hooks into the top bale, caught it on his thigh, and heaved it up to Nash, who put it into place.

"There's not much room left up here," he called down.

"Let's call it good, then. I'll feed the others in the next few days."

Nash bounded down from the rafters where he'd been stacking bales. His muscles shook, and he was drenched with sweat from working inside the hot wooden barn. The still air was filled with dust and the scent of fresh hay—and sweat-drenched men.

"Fuck it's hot in here. I don't know how you did it by yourself."

"It takes me a couple of days. I appreciate the help. It made it a lot easier." Luke buried the hooks into a bale about head high and motioned Nash ahead of him. He sighed as the breeze hit him. A movement caught his eye and he realized Luke was stripping off his sweat-soaked T-shirt. Nash was mesmerized as taut muscle appeared along with the sweat-matted hair over his chest and stomach. The heat flowing through Nash had nothing to do with the blazing Oklahoma sun.

When Luke locked his fingers behind his neck, exposing a matted and wet mass of dark hair under each arm, Nash's desire flamed and a moan slipped from his lips. Luke spun toward him to find Nash frozen in place.

"You okay?"

Nash closed the distance between them. He stopped an arm's length from Luke and stared at his hard body. Their eyes met and Nash grinned. "Damn."

"Sorry, I sweat like a pig. And the hair doesn't help."

Nash lifted his hand toward Luke until he could feel the heat against his palm. He stared intently as Luke swallowed hard. Taking that as permission, he ran his hands over Luke's masculine chest.

Luke seemed unable to move as Nash pushed his hand harder, the texture flowing under his palms lighting all his nerves. He skipped his touch higher, clasped one bicep, and squeezed it. The smell of hard work and musk filled Nash's nose and mouth. His body responded, and he moaned again.

"I'm gonna stink. It was really hot in there."

"You smell good enough to eat to me."

A tremor ran through Luke's body. "What're you gonna do?"

Not saying a word, Nash pressed his face into Luke's armpit and inhaled. His cock was so hard it hurt as he began eating out Luke's pit. He ran his tongue over it. Switching to the other arm, he repeated his actions. The breeze flowed over their steaming bodies as Nash wiped his mouth on his arm.

"Shit, that was damn fine."

"I can't believe you like my pits."

"You like feet, I like pits. Everybody likes something; you charge more for some."

Luke smirked at Nash. "What?"

"Never mind. But damn you turn me on."

Before Luke could reply, Nash wrapped an arm around Luke's bare waist and pulled them against each other. He kissed Luke passionately while he ground his crotch against Luke's. The combination soon had Nash on the edge of losing his load. He also realized Luke was being particularly passive through this whole thing. He nipped at Luke's bottom lip, then pulled away slowly.

"You okay? I can stop. You just look like a damn wet dream."

"You shouldn't mess with people. No one likes to be made fun of. I know I'm short and hairy. When I was in eighth grade, they said I looked like an Ewok."

Nash was shocked. *How do I get Luke to believe me?* He traced his fingers over the scruff on Luke's cheek. "I hate to break this to you, but you aren't really that hairy. I've seen guys with tons more body hair. You have the perfect amount to be hot and sexy as hell."

Luke turned red, looked down, and started digging the toe of his boot into the dirt.

"What?"

"I just. Nothing. Really it's embarrassing and stupid."

Nash ran his fingers around the back of Luke's neck and brought their foreheads together. The scent wafting off Luke hit him again, but he fought it down this time. "What don't you want to tell me now?"

Luke blushed even deeper, his ears hot in Nash's hand. "Nothing. Can we drop it?"

"Nope. I never let someone off the hook."

"Bobby said it was gross."

Nash sighed. "And we've already established that Bobby is a complete fucking idiot. So what?"

"All right, all right. I have a hairy butt."

"Like, how hairy?" Nash leered at Luke.

"I don't know! It feels hairy. Bo—someone told me it was hairy."

Nash grinned mischievously, dropped his hands to Luke's ass, and squeezed. He leaned in and whispered in Luke's ear. "Let me see."

"Really?"

Nash spun Luke around and squatted behind him. He tugged at the jeans, but they could have been glued to Luke for all the movement he got. He reached around and popped open the buttons.

Luke squealed and grabbed his pants to keep them from falling down. "Hey! Someone could catch us. We can't do this in broad daylight."

"That's part of the excitement. The chance of getting caught." Nash leaned close and nipped at his butt before he stood, wrapped his arms around Luke, and nuzzled against the back of his neck. "The barn looks pretty private."

"The barn?"

Nash could tell Luke's resolve was melting. He ran one hand higher on Luke's chest and rolled his nipple between his fingers. He pushed the other hand south and started teasing the hard bulge in his jeans.

Luke might have lasted two minutes before he grabbed Nash's arm and dragged him to the hay barn. They sprinted through the door, and Nash slammed Luke into the wall of green rectangles of hay while he kissed him frantically.

68

Without a word, he pinned Luke against the bales and tugged down his jeans to reveal a pair of skintight white compression shorts stretched to contain a hard dick. Nash grabbed the top of the shorts and began peeling them off. Inch by inch Luke's shaft appeared until the tip of his thick cock strained against the waist of the shorts. With a final tug, it slipped free and swung out.

"Sweet fucking cock."

"Yeah, so you keep saying."

Nash grinned and leaned to one side, pulling a condom from his back pocket. He ripped the packet open and unrolled it down Luke in an instant. He pressed the latex-sheathed cock against Luke's hard stomach and flicked his tongue along the underside as he worked lower and lower. Soft squeaking noises leaked into the hot barn air as he sucked one of Luke's nuts into his mouth and coated it with spit. First one and then the other, he sucked Luke's balls.

Then he had to know. He grabbed Luke's hips and twisted him around. The white shorts still clung to the crest of his butt. Luke's dark tan stopped at the top. With a snap, he exposed Luke's ass.

"Well?"

Nash could hear the plea in Luke's voice. He leaned in and kissed each cheek. "You have a hot fucking ass, like the rest of you. It's perfect."

"But…."

"No buts. Hot. Fucking. Ass."

Nash dug through his pockets, but the other condom packets were gone. All of them. He thought back through the day—it must have been the ride. Nash struggled with the code he'd lived with that had kept him alive over all the years: no protection, no sex. Rimming was low risk, he reasoned to himself. And what about Luke? He'd only been with one person. He traced his finger along Luke's buttcheek, and the moan that resulted decided it.

He pried apart Luke's cheeks. The musk surrounded Nash and his desire for Luke rocketed. All inhibitions were thrown to the winds and Nash pressed his face against the prime butt in front of him. He flicked his tongue along the trench until he found his goal.

Driving his tongue against the tight pucker, Nash licked and tasted the delicious man pinned in front of him. Luke moaned and pushed back against Nash. Accepting the invitation, Nash sank his tongue inside. As he plunged deeper, he found himself wanting more. He leaned back, gasping for air, to watch Luke's entrance pulse.

"Fuck, you're hot."

"So good. Feels so amazing."

Nash slipped his finger down Luke's spit-soaked cleft, rubbing it against his hole to a chorus of new groans. He circled slowly, enjoying the passionate sounds filling the barn.

"Do it. Put it in. Don't be a tease."

Luke's plea shocked Nash back to reality. He'd been dangerously close to deserting his rules and barebacking with Luke. He'd never been willing to do that, and he'd been offered plenty of incentives to say yes. Nash chided himself.

"Can't, stud. I lost the other condoms on the ride." He spun Luke back around and ran his tongue up the underside of Luke's cock. As he reached the crown, he kissed it and grinned.

"You ready to come, cowboy?"

"Please. I'm so close."

Nash pressed his mouth over Luke's latex-covered cock, enjoying his lips stretching around it. It bumped the back of his throat and pressed farther. He worked for a minute and then sank lower until his lips were buried in Luke's bush.

"Ah, fuck! Damn!"

Luke's cries of pleasure drove Nash further. He slipped his head upward until his lips were tightly clamped around his cockhead, then slid down all the way. With each movement, he gained speed and Luke's cries became less and less coherent. His muscles tightened under Nash's grip and he knew they were getting close.

With a groan that sounded of pure lust, Luke grabbed Nash's head and started face fucking him. He ran his hands over Luke's sweaty torso as the thrusts came hard and fast. As Luke reached a fever pitch, Nash grabbed his nipples and twisted them.

"Fuck!"

Luke's body tensed before beginning to shake. The muscle contractions were so strong Nash could count them. He groaned a final time and grabbed Nash's shoulders for support. Nash sucked the softening cock deep inside again before slowly sliding off.

Luke lifted Nash to his feet and kissed him tenderly. "That was mind-blowing."

"Good. That was kind of my goal."

"My turn." Luke started to kneel but Nash caught his shoulder. "I wasn't lying. I don't have another condom, and we really should be careful."

"Hand job is careful, right?"

Nash's cock flexed in his pants. "Yeah, a hand job is pretty safe."

Luke kissed him again and then turned Nash so his back was leaning against Luke's chest. The texture against him sent more flames of lust. When Luke grabbed his nipple rings and tugged, he thought he would come. The passion was building when Luke stopped and dropped his hands to Nash's crotch.

He squeezed Nash's rock-hard cock and chuckled. "It's nice to see it wasn't just me."

"No, stud. It wasn't just you. You've had me like that for the whole time."

"Well let's see if little Nash wants to play."

Before he could reply, Luke had opened his jeans and slipped a hand inside. Nash's clever retort turned into a strangled gasp as Luke tugged on the PA ring. Luke jerked on it again and it was like someone had pulled the pin on a grenade. He was about to explode.

"Luke, fuck! Gonna drop a load, man!"

Luke stroked Nash's cock. He lost himself in his now impending orgasm. As forming thoughts became beyond his ability, he absently watched as Luke leaned forward and let saliva drip onto his cock. Luke tightened his grip and stroked slowly.

With each caress, he would slide until his hand ground against Nash's crotch, then ease upward, twisting his fist around the deep red head of Nash's dick. His muscles slowly tensed until the first shot leapt from his cock to leave a thick white line on the ground. Nash lost himself in the washes of euphoria that roiled over him. With a final tightening, the last evidence of his orgasm oozed from his cock.

"Holy fuck."

Luke kissed Nash's back as he milked the last of his come. He shuddered again, then twisted to give Luke another kiss. "That was amazing. You aren't supposed to be the one who does mind-fucking sex."

Luke chuckled softly as he ran his hands over Nash. "I've had plenty of practice jacking off. I should be good at it."

Nash froze in silence for a moment before bursting out laughing. "I can't believe you admitted to beating off."

"Hey, you know what they say. Ninety-five percent of guys do it, and the other five percent lie."

A comfortable warmth crept through his body. A feeling of satisfaction that he hadn't felt since he was fifteen. Another kiss landed on the side of his neck.

"I think we better clean up. This isn't exactly private." He grabbed Nash's jeans and pulled them up. When he reached down to close Nash's zipper, he paused for an instant and ran his little finger through the ring in Nash's cock, turning it. "This is cool. But I don't know what to do with it."

Nash groaned and bit down on Luke's earlobe. "Knock it off or we'll be starting all over again."

CHAPTER SEVEN

NASH STUMBLED into the kitchen as Luke poured himself a glass of milk and took a sip. This time there was no conversation as Nash shuffled across the floor to the coffeemaker. He pulled a cup the size of a soup bowl from the cabinet and filled it with the steaming black liquid. Once he'd managed to down about half, he motioned with it toward Luke.

"What are you dressed up for?"

"Church."

Luke drank more of his milk while they stared at each other. The tension grew until Luke broke it. "You can go with me if you'd like. I swear they don't sacrifice a chicken every full moon." A grin filled Luke's face as he motioned at Nash's naked crotch. "You would have to dress up a little more."

Nash's jaw clenched and relaxed before he took another drink. Once he lowered the cup, he stared into Luke's eyes. "Churches and I don't really get along. I don't need anyone telling me that I'm going to hell. I already know."

"It's not like that. It's an Episcopal Church and is gay friendly. The reverend is supportive too. It's a cool place." Nash's expression hardened. "I know, I know. I grew up going to one of those judgmental churches too. But I think it's good to have some time each week to calm down and chill."

Luke pulled out the real reason he thought Nash might agree to go. "There's an outstanding coffee shop close too. They have fantastic crepes. Gourmet coffee, not the stuff I get at Walmart."

"Crepes? In the sticks of Oklahoma?"

"I swear to you. They're fantastic. My treat."

Nash seemed to be wavering.

"It's too late. I can't get dressed in time."

"Jump in the shower. I'll get you some clothes out."

"I don't have time to fix my hair."

"Pull it back into a ponytail. It'll be fine."

"Well, fuck."

Happiness flooded Luke, but he only let a small grin show. He finished his glass of milk, walked over, and spun Nash toward the bathroom. He put a hand on each shoulder and pushed him forward.

"Hurry up. I'll look through your bag and lay out some clothes."

"Okay, I guess that'll work."

Once Luke heard the shower running, he grabbed Nash's bag and hefted it to the bed. He slid the zipper open and lifted carefully folded pairs of pants onto the bed. Luke hadn't paid that much attention, but now he realized the clothes were immaculately clean and in some cases almost invisibly patched, but far from new. Much of the heavy embroidery on the back pockets of the jeans Nash wore had been carefully repaired.

Toward the bottom of the bag he found a black shirt that looked like it would fit a seventh grader and a matching pair of pants. The material was slick under Luke's touch. It certainly wasn't like anything he'd ever worn.

As he considered the clothing he'd laid out, the shower turned off and Nash walked in, toweling his hair. Completely uninhibited, he dried himself while Luke made a final selection.

"Did you want me to get you some underwear?"

Nash chuckled as he pulled on the shirt Luke laid out for him. "You'd have a hard time finding them since I don't own any."

Heat washed over Luke. "Oh. Okay. I'll clean up the kitchen while you're getting dressed." Soft laughter followed Luke as he escaped the room.

He was focused so intently on cleaning the kitchen that he almost dropped the plate he was putting away when Nash appeared beside him.

"Holy crap! You scared the bejeezus out of me!"

"Sorry. But we have a problem, Houston."

"What's wrong?"

"The only shoes I've got are biker boots, sneakers, or flip-flops. I don't think they'll work for what you have in mind."

"What size do you wear?"

"Ten and a half."

Luke took off toward his room. "Hang on."

He returned with a pair of black boots that he held out to Nash. "These should fit. We wear the same size."

Nash dropped to the floor where he stood and pulled on the boots. A few seconds later he was back on his feet, walking around like a kid with a new toy. Joy built inside Luke at being able to make Nash happy.

"These are cool. They aren't like boots to go clubbing in."

"No, they're Ropers. You can have 'em. I have new ones."

"These look new," Nash said.

"Nah, I've had them for years. You can have 'em."

Nash turned each foot and the light played off their brightly polished surface. He arched an eyebrow but didn't say a word as they made their way to the pickup. The trip through the rolling hills and peacefully grazing livestock to Tahlequah was largely quiet as Luke thought about the past few days. He glanced over as they got closer, but Nash stared out the window, expressionless. Luke was conflicted with how he felt about the tall, handsome man riding with him, but he knew he'd laughed more in the past few days than in as many months before.

As they parked outside the church, Nash turned to Luke. "You know, if I burst into flames, I'm blaming you."

"Don't sweat it. I walk in and out and you can barely smell the brimstone."

Nash looked like he was being sent to the inquisition, and Luke swore Nash's legs were quaking before they'd traveled half the distance to the unique ground-hugging building. They entered the sanctuary and the jewel tones of the sun through the stained glass relaxed Luke as it always did. He hoped Nash felt the same way.

The next hour went as well as Luke could have hoped. At first, Nash fidgeted almost as much as the ten-year-old beside them, but as the service progressed, he seemed to relax. By the time church ended, he sang with the rest of the congregation. As they worked their way out, he leaned close to Luke.

"It wasn't as bad as I remembered."

"Good. Then we'll get some lunch and maybe do some sightseeing."

He turned back in time to see the person in front of them wrapped in a bear hug by the reverend. Luke had forgotten to warn Nash about their enthusiastic pastor.

"Luke! I'm so glad to see you today." And he was enveloped in a tight embrace. Typically he didn't mind the display at all. Luke usually left with a warm, contented feeling. Today his tension was high because of his concern about Nash.

The reverend released one of his arms and pulled Nash into the hug, much to Luke's surprise.

"I'm so glad you brought your boyfriend with you. It's nice to finally meet him."

Shock reverberated through his system. Who in the world was he talking about and how was he going to explain it to Nash? But when he looked at Nash, he grinned at both of them.

Nash ran an arm around Luke's waist and pulled them together. "It's great to meet you too, sir. Luke talks about you all the time."

He patted their shoulders and ushered them along. "You boys enjoy your day."

Before Luke could come up with a reply, Nash gripped his hand and pulled him to the truck. Luke let him, and his apprehension at how he was going to explain this whole misunderstanding made his stomach churn. But as Nash released him, Luke realized he was laughing. Perhaps tinged a little too much with hysteria, but still, laughter.

"I'm sorry about that. I never told him I had a boyfriend."

"Don't sweat it. I never thought I'd see the day when some preacher would welcome me as someone's boyfriend. Never."

The dread lifted as Luke stared into Nash's smiling face. "Yeah, I told you they were accepting." Luke scratched his head and shrugged. "Usually they aren't quite that accepting, though."

"Hey, I went in a church and didn't burst into flames. I'll call it good." He locked eyes with Luke and lifted an eyebrow. "Now, where is this fantastic coffee shop with crepes to die for?"

"Well, now. I don't think I ever said they were to die for. But they're good."

They climbed into the pickup and a few minutes later were parking outside the coffee shop. They sat in the truck and Luke considered his options. He turned to Nash and tried to explain again.

Nash motioned Luke into silence. "Don't sweat it. You don't strike me as the type to lie."

"It's not like I told them I was shopping for a boyfriend online."

Nash chuckled and glanced at Luke. "But you kind of were."

Heat pulsed through Luke, leaving him lost for words.

"Look, I'm fine with people saying I'm your boyfriend. I've been called a lot worse. Relax. If I have a problem with something, I'll tell you. Deal?"

"Deal. Sorry about all the drama, but this is so new for me."

"Chill. It'll be fine."

Luke threw up his hands in surrender, jumped out of the pickup, and headed into the small cafe with Nash right beside him.

They stood back, studying the menu board. "What's good?"

"Everything I've had was delicious. I was thinking the chipotle, though."

"That sounds outstanding, but so does the pesto one."

Luke unconsciously slid his hand up Nash's back and squeezed his neck. "What if we get both and share?"

Nash grinned at Luke. "I think it's a little late to worry about swapping germs, so that works fine for me."

Luke chuckled as he stepped up and placed their order. Their lunch was brought out almost before they found a place to sit. Nash sipped his coffee and sighed.

"Ah, damn. That's good. Nothing personal." He looked over at Luke's glass. "What'd you get?"

"Iced chai. It's a good thing you can't get 'em in Stillwell, or I'd be broke all the time."

He cut off a bite of his crepe, scooped it up on his fork, and held the piece toward Nash. "Here. Try it and tell me what you think."

Instead of taking the fork like Luke expected, Nash leaned forward and let Luke feed him. He chewed for a while before nodding. "It's delicious. A little heat but not too much. Yeah, I like that." Nash cut off a bite from the crepe he'd chosen and fed it to Luke.

"Oh yeah, I love that. The pesto's so good. You can tell they make it fresh."

They continued their meal, sharing the food and enjoying each other's company. Luke noticed the two college guys sitting near the window looking at them from time to time. They didn't look particularly threatening, typical college kids, so he put them out of his mind to enjoy the conversation.

"That was good. Anything else we should do while we're in town?"

"We're close to Northeastern's campus. We could wander around the grounds for a little while if you'd like."

There was a loud bang as the college guys slammed their trays down on the counter. Everyone's gaze turned to the pair and one of them nodded at Luke and Nash. "If you're gonna let them in here, we won't be back."

The horrified expression on the girl's face was echoed by others when Luke glanced around the room. But the number of heads nodding in agreement were far more disturbing. His chest constricted, and he felt as if he'd been gut punched.

"I'm ready to go. How about you?" Luke asked.

"Seems like a good time to exit stage left."

Once they stepped outside, Luke took a deep breath, fighting the same feelings of being the outcast that he'd battled through junior high and high school. Then he felt a squeeze on his shoulder and glanced over to see Nash.

"It happens everywhere. You can't get the stupid out of some people. Lunch was great. Let's walk through the campus you were talking about."

Luke nodded and silently walked in the direction of the university. Nash slipped his hand down his back and eased the tips of his fingers into the back of his black jeans. Luke was glad for the contact; it gave him comfort he hadn't experienced in years. As they made their way deeper into campus, he took Luke's hand in his and gave it a little squeeze.

Luke was surprised when Nash continued to hold his hand. When they came upon a large bronze statue, Nash turned to him.

"Who's that?"

"Sequoyah."

"Like the trees?"

"Actually, I think the trees are named after him. He created the Cherokee alphabet. They used to have a newspaper printed in Cherokee."

"Really? That's cool. They're a native tribe, right?"

Luke grinned, realizing how easy it was to grow up with something and think it was common knowledge. "They've lived here for a couple hundred years, but they moved here from the south. Have you heard of the Trail of Tears?"

"I think so. Maybe in elementary." The tension built. "I never finished high school. Let's go. This is stupid."

He dropped Luke's hand and started toward the pickup. Luke trotted to catch up. Trying desperately to regain their moment of quiet, he blurted out the first thing that came into his head.

"Did you know the Cherokee have Two-Spirits?"

Nash slowed but didn't stop. After a few more steps, he asked, "What's Two-Spirits?"

"People that have their identity from both sexes. They believe it was a sign of someone who would be a spirit person. You know, a medicine man kind of thing."

"So they thought gay people were special?"

"A friend of mine whose grandmother is Cherokee told me. She said gay is a white thing. The Cherokee don't have the same idea of who you have sex with. At least the old beliefs said that."

Nash stopped and glanced at Luke. "That's pretty cool. Not like it is nowadays. It would be nice for everyone to think we're not really any different."

Luke nodded in agreement. "Yeah. It would be." He glanced at Nash before continuing. "Wanna finish looking over the campus?"

"Sure. I guess so." Nash looked away from Luke as if searching for something. "Do they have an art department?"

"Yeah, I think so. And an art gallery somewhere."

Their eyes met. "I think I'd like to see those places."

THE RETURN trip to Luke's home had been quiet. Not stressful or tense, it just seemed they both were thinking about the day. Sundays Nash typically slept until early afternoon and then nursed a strong cup of coffee while he flipped through the paper. He'd certainly never get up in the early morning and go to church. He'd had his fill of church.

"You're being really quiet. Sorry about the deal in the coffee shop."

Nash waved a dismissive hand at Luke and shook his head. "No, those two are assholes. You can't get worked up over assholes."

"What, then? You look like you've been thinking about something."

"Church."

"What about it?"

"I haven't been since I left home. I swore I'd never set foot in one again. But it wasn't bad. Kind of relaxing."

"Yeah, it's pretty good. They seem okay with gay people in the congregation too. When I first started attending, I think a few people quit. I actually talked to the minister about it. I wanted him to know I'd understand if they didn't want me in the congregation."

"What'd he say?"

Luke scratched his head, then shrugged. "He said that was the member's choice to stay or not, but the church's role was to welcome everyone."

Nash snorted but didn't share what he was thinking. He had enough baggage with churches to last the rest of his life.

Luke began again. "Not buying it yet, huh?"

"Sorry. It's…. Well, as they say, it's complicated."

"It's okay, I understand."

When they turned into Luke's driveway, Nash realized their conversation had gone on for quite some time. He followed Luke into the house and went into his bedroom to change. He carefully folded the shirt and pants back into his bag and found some of the more worn clothes in case Luke needed help. He pulled off the boots and stared at them. He couldn't afford what they cost, and they wouldn't fit into his life once he was back in Atlanta.

The fantasy had been that, a fantasy. Find a guy, fall in love, and live happily ever after. But he knew it didn't work like that. Eventually it would all fall apart, and he'd be back selling his ass to guys wanting something they couldn't get at home.

He turned the boot over and over in his hand. He should give them back to Luke and tell him his fantasy man was a hooker. But he wasn't ready. The make-believe was his own this time, and he wasn't quite willing to have it go up in flames. He pulled a threadbare shirt from his bag and began carefully wiping the dust from the boots. He meticulously went over each one until they were back to the condition they'd been in when Luke gave them to him. He carefully sat them beside the bed, then slipped his feet into a pair of flip-flops and went in search of Luke.

Locating him didn't take long. Nash had barely cleared the door when he heard noise from the kitchen. He joined Luke in time to see him slip a huge pan into the oven.

"Holy shit, what are you cooking?"

Luke waved a piece of paper in the air. "It's from Chris. She said if you had to eat any more of my cooking I'd probably run you off. So she made lasagna, garlic bread, and a salad."

The scent of the lasagna filled the room, and Nash drooled in anticipation. He glanced over to Luke and discovered he was being watched.

"Don't worry. I have detailed instructions on how to heat it. Chris says it's Luke proof."

"I didn't have any complaints about your cooking."

Luke chuckled. "Now you're being nice. Even I get tired of my cooking. And the choice of places to eat around here isn't huge."

"Well, Italian is a favorite. So Chris's cooking won't go to waste. I hate that she had to make the trip all the way out here, though."

Luke glanced at Nash, his brows furrowed. Then they shot upward. "Oh! No, Chris lives on the next farm up the road. Quarter mile or so. Her mom lives in town, and Chris checks on her all the time."

"Chris lives by herself?"

"Yeah. Her brother was killed in a riding accident when we were in high school. His horse bucked and pitched him into a ravine. He hit his head when he landed." He gave Nash a significant look. "Don't say anything about it. It about killed Chris. She's pulled my butt out of enough scrapes, and I don't want to bring back any painful memories."

"Of course, Chris seems cool. I wouldn't want to hurt her."

"Thanks." Luke looked like he was about to say something when the timer went off. "Hey, if you'll grab some plates, I'll put the garlic bread in the oven and we'll be ready to eat in a few minutes."

A little later they were digging into the huge squares of lasagna that Luke dished up for each of them, along with a couple of pieces of garlic bread and some salad. Nash had eaten almost half the food on his plate before he realized Luke was toying with his meal.

"What's up?"

"Hmm, do you like it?"

"Yeah, it's delicious. Why? You're not eating."

Luke smiled shyly. "I was nervous." He cut off a bit and popped it into his mouth.

Nash swallowed what he was eating and shook his head. "You goof. If I'm eating it, I'm liking it."

Luke's cheeks turned pink, and he shrugged. "I wasn't sure."

"Eat. Stop worrying. Besides, you said Chris cooked this. Why are you all worried about me liking it?"

Luke's face turned an interesting color of red. He looked so sheepish Nash couldn't help but laugh. "You cooked it, didn't you? And were going to blame poor Chris if I didn't like it?"

"Not exactly."

Nash chuckled as he finished a second bite and swallowed. He gave Luke an impish grin. "Then what 'exactly' did you do?"

"Okay, okay. I put it together last week and Chris kept it in her freezer. She brought it over when she left to go into town to check on her mother."

"I'll buy that. And you can stop worrying. Your lasagna is really good."

The rest of the meal was quiet and companionable. Nash ran the crust of his bread through the last bit of sauce on his plate and tossed it into his mouth, savoring every flavor in the homemade meal.

He leaned back and groaned. "Man, that was good. I can't remember the last time I had lasagna as tasty."

"There's dessert too." Luke grinned when Nash groaned.

"Oh, hell no. You're already fattening me up. I'm stuffed! They'll tell me how fat I am in Atlanta."

"Fat? You're crazy."

Nash pulled up his shirt to expose his trim waist. He pinched a tiny roll on the side of his stomach. "See? Fat. Soon I'll only get old ugly guys."

The second the words left his mouth he wished them back. He wasn't ready to end the fantasy yet. But what was he going to tell Luke? *Chill. He might not notice. I may be off the hook.*

"What do you mean, only get old men?"

Nash made a decision, probably not his best. He was going to lie like a son of a bitch. "Oh, you know, that old saying when you get the crap jobs at work, you get the old man."

Luke stared at him and shook his head. "I've never heard it before. Must be an Atlanta thing."

"Could be, or some dumb shit thing I learned in Alabama. Who knows?" Nash's gut twisted. He found lying to Luke left him sick to his stomach. He made a change of topic as they started clearing the table. "So what do you want to do tonight? I'm up for whatever."

"How about movies? I thought you might like to watch a mindless flick and have a little relaxation," Luke said.

Nash eased their plates into the dishwasher and flipped it closed. "Sounds like a plan. You're in charge of popcorn and I'll be in charge of cold beer and using my butt to warm the couch."

Luke chuckled and shook his head. "Pick a movie and I'll make us some popcorn."

Nash grabbed beer from the fridge and made his way into the living room. He started through the selection and found a movie he thought would be good mindless entertainment. He slid it into the player as Luke came into the room with a bowl of popcorn that smelled delicious. Nash settled against the end of the couch and patted the cushion beside him. "Plant that cute butt right here."

Luke's cheeks reddened again, but he settled into the seat beside Nash. He leaned up and kissed Luke on the cheek before taking a handful of popcorn. They sat snuggling close as the previews for coming attractions played.

"By the way, where do you keep the good movies?"

Luke's forehead crinkled as he stared at Nash. Then his brows shot upward and he turned crimson. "I don't know what you're talking about."

"Yeah, yeah. Where's the porn stash? I know you have one."

"Porn? I don't got no stinkin' porn."

"Bad impression, but I'll tickle you if I have to."

"Oh, watch the movie and stop mouthing off."

Nash launched himself at Luke and tickled him. In an instant, Luke was laughing hysterically and trying to squirm away from Nash's dancing fingers. Nash enjoyed the feeling of innocent play as he kept up the attack. Luke bucked under him, trying to escape, but gasped helplessly for air. Nash dug his fingers into Luke's pits, and a fresh burst of laughter filled the house.

"Stop! Stop, stop. I give. Calf rope! Stop!"

Nash relented and grinned at Luke as he tried to catch his breath. "No funny business, big guy. Where's your porn stash?"

Luke breathed deeply and looked at Nash, his face one of innocent joy. "Mostly on my laptop. I only have one or two DVDs."

"See, was that so hard?"

Luke collapsed against the couch, his arms over his head. "Oh my God. I was a little kid the last time someone tickled me like that."

"You better watch yourself, buster. I can bring out the tickle monster again."

"Yeah, yeah. Whatever."

Nash slid his fingers over Luke's ribs and he shot upward, chuckling. "Okay! Enough. What movie did you pick?"

"One of the comic book flicks. I didn't think we needed a tear jerker." Nash grabbed Luke's feet and pulled them into his lap.

Luke tensed at the touch, then relaxed, and grinned at Nash. "The sappy ones Chris bought. I like the action movies myself."

"They're both okay with me. But action movies sound more fun tonight."

The pair settled in and arranged themselves on the couch with Luke's feet in Nash's lap. He smirked at the sigh he got when he laid his hands over Luke's feet. A few minutes passed and he eased off Luke's socks and dropped them to the floor.

"What're you doing?"

"I thought you might like a foot rub."

"That's not fair. You know my kryptonite but I don't know yours."

Nash pressed his thumb against the arch of Luke's foot and rubbed. "You'll have to work at finding it, then. It might take you a little effort, though."

Luke sighed and squirmed against the couch. "No fair. You're a cock tease."

"More like a toe tease." Nash ran his hands over Luke's feet. *He really does have hot feet, and I don't have a thing for them either.* Nash caressed the top of Luke's foot and then over the wiry dark hair on his ankles. Smooth twinks usually appealed to him, but Luke brought up emotions he couldn't remember having before.

He slid his gaze to Luke's crotch. The bulge that flexed every so often gave Nash all the information he needed. He was having the effect he wanted. He twisted on the couch, exploring Luke's thick thighs with his hands. He cut his eyes to his hunk and found him propped on his elbows, watching. He slid his hand over the mound in Luke's crotch and the sigh grew in volume. He reached for the button on Luke's jeans, but was surprised when Luke lifted Nash's hands away.

"I know it's a little late to say slow down, but everything you do makes me want you more. I'm afraid all my common sense is going out the window. Because I want to try everything with you. But I need time. Like I said, most of this is new to me."

Nash curled down, put his mouth on the end of the bulge traveling down Luke's leg, and breathed.

Luke grabbed his head and held it for a second before lifting him off. "Oh yeah. I don't have any control when you do stuff. I really want it all, though."

Nash wasn't sure how Luke's refusal made him feel. He'd never had it happen before. Even men he'd dated knew what he did for a living and assumed Nash was ready for whatever they proposed. But Luke didn't know and wanted to slow down.

"Okay, if it'd make you feel better, we can just snuggle tonight."

"Are you pissed?"

Nash grinned at the thought. "Not at all. Maybe a little surprised, I guess. But I see your point."

"You still up for the movie?" Luke asked.

"Of course! For snuggling too. Come here."

86

Luke turned and crawled up the couch. Nash pulled him close and gave him a light kiss. "Relax. You didn't do anything wrong. Let's watch the rest of the movie. We're at the good parts."

The pair settled in against each other, with Luke tucked against Nash's shoulder. By the time the credits played, Luke's head was in Nash's lap and he was gently running his fingers through Luke's hair. The moment was so serene Nash wished it could go on forever. But hard reality told Nash nothing good lasted for very long.

Luke rolled onto his back and looked up at Nash. "Good choice. I'm afraid that's pretty much it for me tonight, though. Tomorrow I have to work a few calves and fix some fence in the back hundred acres."

Nash pushed his fingers through Luke's hair a last time before easing them out. "I can help. If you'd like?"

"Sure! I'd love that. But I know you didn't come here to work."

Nash shrugged. "It's nothing like my life in Atlanta, so it's fun for me. I don't know how much help I'll be, but I'm game."

"I'd love to have some company. It's a long day when I'm out working on fence."

"Well ask anyone, I can run my mouth."

Luke glanced over at Nash in time for him to stick out his tongue and wiggle it at Luke. "Not exactly what I had in mind, but who knows."

Nash climbed off the couch, grabbed Luke's hand, and pulled him up. He cupped the back of Luke's head and pressed their lips together. His tongue darted out and slid along Luke's lips. The kiss built the pressure inside Nash. He pulled back, not ready to admit the depths of what he felt any more than Luke. He slid a finger over Luke's scruffy jaw and grinned.

"We do this any more and I'm going to throw you down for wild monkey sex."

Luke ran his rough hand over Nash's smooth cheek. "I'm not sure what wild monkey sex is, but I'm pretty sure I outweigh you."

"You never can tell. Horny helps me move faster." Nash grinned and leaned into Luke again, nuzzling against his ear. "Night. Hope you sleep well."

He walked out of the room and when he glanced back, Luke stood staring in his direction.

Chapter Eight

THE MIDDAY sun beat down from a cloudless sky, baking Luke and everything around him. Dried grasses made a scraping sound against his jeans. He wiped the sweat from his face as Nash stabbed the posthole digger into the hard ground. Luke lifted out the jug of cool water and took a long drink. After standing in the scorching sun, the steady thump, thump, thump of Nash digging a posthole juggled him back to reality.

"Hey, Nash. Come get a drink. You don't wanna overheat."

Nash jabbed the diggers into the dense clay and joined Luke. He took a couple of long drinks, but when he went for a third, Luke stopped him.

"The water'll make you sick if you drink too much while you're hot. You'll be puking all over the place."

Nash handed the jug back with a nod. "Yeah, I knew that. I just forgot."

Luke looked around and chewed on the inside of his cheek. It took a little while to realize what Nash wanted. "I packed some food from the house. We can stop and eat if you want."

Nash beamed at him. "That'd be amazing. I'm starved. We've been at this since the buttcrack of dawn."

Luke choked back a snort as he pulled the little cooler from the bed of the Gator. "I think it was more like seven thirty when we left. But it is close to noon. I could eat too." He paused and looked around before motioning to a patch of grass. "You want to eat there?"

"The rocks might be easier. We could spread out along that ledge."

Luke peered into the deep shadow under the outcropping. "The only problem is snakes would like that too. Gets them out of the sun while it's hot. I'd just as soon not find a big ole rattlesnake."

Nash's next words came out in a much higher voice. "Snakes? The grassy patch is fine."

Luke studied him before cocking his head. "Maybe we should head to the house. I don't want you to get burned again."

"Are we done?"

Luke studied the fence before shaking his head. "No. I was hoping to get to the water gate at the bottom of the hill."

"Then there's no need to stop. We don't want to leave a job half-done."

"You sound like Granddad."

"Well, he was a smart man, then. So here's an idea. Let's eat in the shade of the four-wheel thing. Then we will get some break from the sun but not in snake land."

"It's a Gator, and that sounds like an outstanding plan." Luke plopped down beside the vehicle and rotated the top of the cooler. He glanced inside and looked at Nash hesitantly. "Remember, I can't cook."

"You've been doing fine so far, so don't sweat it. I'd eat about anything at this point."

Luke pulled out a couple of sandwiches and containers of pudding. He offered one of each to Nash. "It's peanut butter and jelly. This morning it sounded pretty good." He hesitated, not wanting to sound any more ridiculous. "The jelly's homemade. The sand plums went crazy this year so Chris and I made jelly."

The nerves that he'd been living with since Nash arrived started acting up again. He'd never felt this combination of dread and longing. *It's a sandwich. Why is it so important for Nash to like the stupid PB&J?* Nash did seem to be enjoying the food; it was certainly disappearing fast enough. Then it registered that Nash was looking at him.

"You wouldn't happen to have milk in there, would you?"

Luke couldn't stop the goofy grin from appearing on his face, and he couldn't have said why it was there. "No milk, but I do have some bottled water."

He handed one of the bottles to Nash and began eating his food, trying not to stare. He was becoming more infatuated with the slender man. He enjoyed Nash's sense of humor, even when he wanted to curl up and hide in embarrassment. If Nash knew how much porn he had on his computer, well, he'd probably leave in disgust. But he seemed to think it was normal, which was certainly not the way Luke was raised.

"Hey, hey. Earth to Luke."

Heat rushed up his neck. "Sorry, I was thinking about what we still needed to do."

"Really? 'Cause I haven't seen too many people blush over driving posts."

He stammered, and Nash chuckled. Luke lowered himself onto the grass and leaned against the Gator. He avoided Nash's gaze as he ate one of the sandwiches.

They soon polished off their lunch, and both of them were finishing the bottles of water. Luke stood and grabbed the tail of his T-shirt but turned to Nash. "I'm getting hot. Would it bother you if I take off my shirt?"

Nash grinned at him. "You've had your dick in my ass. I think we're long past worrying about shirts."

Luke remained silent but pulled the shirt off and tossed it to the vehicle's seat. He slipped on his leather gloves, grabbed the post driver and a couple of T-posts, and headed down the hill.

The sun had dipped much lower in the afternoon sky when they finished repairing the water gate. Luke stuck the shovel into the ground, laced his fingers behind his neck, and stretched. "I think that's enough for one day. The rest of the fence is in good shape. We might ride the horses tomorrow and check some of the cross fencing."

"I get to ride Jack, right?"

Luke chuckled and draped his arm over Nash's shoulders. "Yeah, you can ride the mule. He's probably smarter than I am anyway."

They stood while Luke admired their work. But a little later, Nash moved from under Luke's friendly embrace.

"Sorry," Luke said. "I didn't mean to—"

"Not even close, dude. But if I'd stood with your sweaty pits so close much longer, I couldn't have guaranteed I could behave."

Luke grinned shyly. "That's fair, I guess. I didn't think about it."

"Yeah, your pits are pretty hot."

"That's it. Your thing is sweaty armpits."

Nash started chuckling. "Well, I wouldn't turn yours down. But that's not number one."

"Dang! I thought I had it."

They gathered their tools and climbed the steep bank to the ATV. By the time they reached the top, sweat ran down Luke's torso. They quickly tossed everything into the vehicle and headed to the house. The evening breeze picked up and Luke enjoyed it playing over his skin. They'd almost reached home when Nash looked at him and smiled. But for some reason Luke detected a sadness.

"What's wrong?"

"Not a thing. Today was great. I'll remember it for a long time."

"It was fun, but you've got several more days of vacation. I'm sure we'll find some other things to do between now and then."

"Yeah."

Luke glanced over again, but Nash stared into the distance. He tried to think of a way to get Nash to talk. But when they arrived, he slipped into the house without another word. Luke closed the equipment barn and followed.

He heard the sound of the shower from Nash's room and was tempted to strip and join him. But after his speech last night, he felt hypocritical to think about pinning Nash against the shower wall and fucking him senseless, which was exactly what he wanted to do.

With his cock half-hard, Luke made his way to the laundry room and stripped, leaving his dirty clothes in a pile he'd take care of later. He had walked back into the living room when a wolf whistle cut through the air.

"Damn! You are grade A prime beef."

Luke jumped and spun to find Nash standing at the door rubbing a towel through his hair. Luke couldn't help but admire the tattoo that covered one arm to just below his elbow and continued down the side of his body to swirl across one buttcheek. The gleaming bits of metal through his nipples and cock turned Luke on in ways he'd never expected.

"I was just…." Luke pointed toward his room.

"Yeah, me too. I'm trying to behave, but you're making it fucking hard."

"Sorry. I didn't mean to."

Nash waved him into silence. "Hey, it works for me."

With that information, Luke was afraid of what he might do and shot into his room to shower. A minute later he eased under the steaming water and sighed as the hot spray loosened his tight muscles. Part of him kept expecting Nash to appear at the door, and there was a certain appeal to having someone chasing after him. But Luke was drying off before he heard Nash's voice coming from the other room.

"I'm starved. Are we eating here or what?"

Luke pulled on a fitted T-shirt, a tight pair of briefs followed by a pair of jeans that left little to the imagination. If he'd been asked about his choices, he would have been unable to explain.

When he walked into the living room, he let out a low whistle at the sight in front of him. "You look hot."

Nash spun toward him, and Luke studied each inch of his body. He was also wearing a tight pullover shirt, but with a hot pair of camouflage pants with pockets down each leg and a pair of lace-up boots that went almost to his knees. He looked like a hotter-than-hell military fantasy.

"You think so?"

"Oh yeah. You'll be fighting them off."

"Will I have to fight you off too?"

A wave of heat washed across Luke's face, and a tendril of sweat ran down his cheek. "Maybe."

"Good, then it's working."

Luke's jaw dropped and he got a grin from Nash. "Now, where are we eating? One of us is getting hungry."

"I was thinking the pizza buffet in town. You can eat until you pop."

"Fattening me up again. I swear, you're trying to get me too chunky to get on the plane back to Atlanta."

Luke stepped closer and brushed his hand over Nash's torso. "You're so far from fat it's not even funny."

Nash chuckled, ran his hand up Luke's back, and rubbed his neck. Each time his fingers touched Luke, it felt like hundreds of little fires blossomed on his skin. A sigh escaped from Luke, and he stepped away.

"Okay, let's go eat. I'm starved too."

He made his way to the door and opened it, motioning Nash through. As he walked past, Nash smiled, and Luke felt a fluttering that was becoming familiar. The rest of the trip whizzed past, and far too quickly, Luke pulled into the parking lot.

"Dammit!"

"What?"

"Bobby's here. I guess we should go somewhere else."

Nash sat silently for a moment before turning to Luke. "Why? You have every right to be here too."

"I know, but I don't want to make it uncomfortable."

"For who? I don't think you owe Bobby-small-dick anything at all."

Luke considered saying something but paused. The seconds ticked past with him sitting unmoving. Someone honked at him and he started forward again. This time he pulled into a parking spot and killed the pickup. "I think I'd love pizza buffet tonight."

Nash grinned, and the two of them made their way into the restaurant. The familiar smells of Luke's favorite pizza drew them into the room. It didn't take long to make their way through the variety of food and search for a place to sit. Luke headed for an empty table and stiffened. His heart sank. The seat he'd been going toward was next to Bobby and his family. He tried to pull himself together, but he wasn't sure he was ready to sit next to his ex and make nice. He considered sitting there anyway when Nash pulled him in another direction.

"There's not letting him run you off, then there's fucking ridiculous. Sitting next to him is ridiculous."

The tension drained from Luke as they made their way to a different table. They filled their plates and ate quietly for a while. When he had refilled his plate for the third time, he heard a chuckle from Nash.

"What?"

"You've got a healthy appetite."

Luke froze with the pizza halfway to his mouth but eased it back onto his plate. "I guess I have kinda porked out. Sorry."

Nash laid his hand on Luke's and squeezed it. "I was teasing. You're all muscle and work hard. It takes a lot of fuel."

A commotion across the restaurant drew their attention. It was Bobby and his family. Something had upset his youngest, and she was screaming at the top of her lungs. It went on until they left. He turned back to find Nash watching him and looking thoughtful. Luke ducked his head. "Sorry. I was wondering what's wrong with Ella."

Nash brushed the concern aside. "Nah, no problem. Bobby seems so familiar, like I should know him." He shrugged and speared another mouthful of salad. "Probably someone from Atlanta looks similar. You know, the whole doppelganger thing."

"I don't know where else you'd've seen him. He's pretty tied up with the bank, and his kids have stuff all the time." Luke's chest constricted, and he dropped his head. "I guess I know a little too much about them, don't I? Sorry about that."

Nash waved his fork in the air. "It happens. Breakups take time, especially when you can't keep from seeing the other person. But you didn't let him run you off. That's good."

"I suppose."

They enjoyed the rest of their meal in relative quiet. Luke was at a loss for words and fought to keep from dwelling on Bobby. He was a miserable failure. He wasn't sure what Nash was thinking, but he kept staring at the door and narrowing his eyes. Luke decided he needed to try to salvage the evening.

"I'm pretty full, but I was thinking we could get some ice cream, head to the house, and relax."

"More food?"

Luke grinned and shrugged. "Of course not. Ice cream is dessert, not food."

"Ah, so that's your logic. I guess I could go for a little. Like a cone or something."

"Sounds like a plan to me."

LUKE MADE several turns until suddenly they were on the highway, heading away from town. The silence lingered, but it was a companionable quiet. They had traveled several miles when Nash turned to Luke.

"Where are we going? I thought we were going to get some ice cream."

"We are, but I wanted to take you to my favorite ice cream place. The closest one is in Sallisaw, which is a few miles south of here. But that will give the pizza time to settle."

Nash sat quietly but then turned to Luke with a grin. "It's pretty dark out here. I think you're taking me out to have your way with me."

Luke chuckled, but his only reply was a quick smile. The road dipped and turned before topping a hill, and he could see city lights spread out before them. Soon they were winding their way through the drive-through window. He turned to Nash with a grin.

"You feeling brave? I'll order for you."

Nash motioned his hand and nodded toward Luke. "I'm at your tender mercy, kind sir."

Luke was practically giddy as he turned to the speaker. "We need two double dips of black walnut ice cream. In a waffle cone."

He listened as they repeated the order, then pulled forward. Luke grinned. "You'll like it. I promise."

"I'm sure it will be amazing."

In short order they were wheeling their way back to the ranch, each of them licking at the ice cream balled in their cones. Nash seemed focused on the cold dessert as they wound down the dark road toward the house. Luke glanced over to see Nash's eyebrows knotted in thought.

"What's up? You're really quiet. The ice cream isn't *that* good."

Nash shot him a grin. "The ice cream is wonderful. I love the black walnut flavor." Nash hesitated. "Something about Bobby makes me think I've seen him. Probably just me being all OCD."

They rolled to a stop in front of the house, and he turned to Nash. "I don't know where you'd have seen him. So far as I know he's never been to Atlanta. There is some conference he goes to in Georgia, but it's in College Park."

Nash's face twitched a few times, but he only nodded. Luke realized the ice cream was dripping onto his hand. He stuck the last bite of cone into his mouth and began licking his fingers clean. He'd sucked on a finger for a second before he realized Nash was staring at him and grinning.

"I guess I look pretty redneck. I probably don't know how to act around people."

"I don't know about other people. But if you keep sucking on your finger like that, I'll give you something bigger to play with."

Luke felt like he stood in front of a bonfire, and he was sure his nipples were about to poke through his shirt. He pulled the tail up to dry his now clean fingers.

"I better take care of the horses before it gets much later. They'll be bitching if they don't get fed pretty soon." Luke jumped out of the pickup and headed to the corral without looking back. He was mortified that he kept doing stupid things in front of Nash. He was sure the handsome young man would leave and never think about Luke again, other than as a funny story to tell his friends. The freak from backwoods Oklahoma. He heard Nash running to catch up. He stopped, turning back to tell Nash he didn't have to hang around if he didn't want to, but was surprised at the first thing Nash said.

"Can I feed Jack?"

Luke flapped his mouth open and closed a few times before shrugging. "I suppose so. He's pretty easy, though. He'll eat about anything."

Nash draped his arm over Luke's shoulder as they walked to the animals, then leaned in to give him a peck on the cheek. "You're really hot. Do you know that?"

Luke stopped and stared at Nash. "Are you trying to embarrass me again? I know I'm just a hick. You really don't have to point it out."

Nash recoiled, looking shocked. "No, not at all. I'm sorry if my teasing bothers you. I'll try to lay off, but I tend to joke with the people I like more than anyone else."

Luke studied Nash before shaking his head. "I guess I'm kinda hypersensitive. No one tells me I'm cute and is serious. Bobby always said I was the best he could find in this one-horse town."

Nash's jaw clenched as he pulled Luke in for a tight hug. He released him, kissed his ear, and whispered, "Bobby was messing with you. In Atlanta you'd never have to buy yourself a drink, and you'd have your pick of men. You're not a twink, but not everyone wants a hairless wonder covered with body glitter."

Luke locked eyes with Nash, his heart thundering. "And do you like twinks?"

With a grin, Nash stepped back and pulled up Luke's shirt and exposed his chest. He ran his fingers through the dark curls. "This is perfect. Looking at you makes me want to jump your ass."

Luke's heart pounded in his ears and his cock stretched down the leg of his pants. "I might let you too. But we gotta take care of the animals first."

Luke carefully measured out food for the horses. He nodded toward the stack of hay. "Would you grab a few flakes of alfalfa too?"

"Sure." Nash grabbed an armload and followed Luke into the pens. The horses and Jack came running to them to stick their noses in the bucket. "Okay, guys! Let me get it in the pans."

Luke trotted to the first of the black tubs and dumped some feed into it. He ran across the arena and repeated the action for each horse.

He'd spread out the pans so that no feed tub was close to another. Glancing back, he yelled to Nash, "Throw a flake on top of each one. They're used to eating together like this so you shouldn't have any problems. But if a couple of them are going at each other, don't get between them."

Nash had gotten hay into about half the tubs when the mule took Nash's hair in his teeth and tugged. He spun around and found Jack meeting him eye to eye. "Mule, you about scared the shit out of me. What the hell are you doing?"

Luke laughed at the exchange between the two. "I think Jack likes you. He never follows me around like that."

Nash held out a handful of hay and chuckled as the mule's soft lips pulled it from his hand. Luke carried the last of the alfalfa to the other feed tubs. Once he was satisfied that the horses were going to play nice, he walked back to Nash. He watched as the mule patiently took bite after bite from Nash's hand.

He glanced toward Luke. "Why do you have him anyway? The horses make sense, you rope with them. But why a mule?"

"Because I'm a pathetic softy."

"That's not really an answer."

"I know. I traded for him. He needed a home. The guy who had Jack couldn't handle him, and I couldn't stand the idea of him being sold off to make dog food or something just as unpleasant."

"Couldn't handle Jack? What the hell? Even I can ride him. He's such a sweetheart, I can't imagine someone wanting to get rid of him."

"Because he lets you. Believe me, if he'd wanted you off, you would have been off, and I don't think he liked his former owner."

Nash rubbed his fingers between the mule's ears as Jack cleaned the last of the hay from his palm before Nash wiped them on his pants. When Nash turned to Luke, he could tell the story had disturbed him even though he was trying to keep a stoic expression.

"Anything else?" Nash asked.

"I think we've pretty much covered it." Luke glanced at Nash. "We can watch a movie again tonight if you'd like. I guess it's kinda boring around here."

"I'm enjoying the quiet. A movie would be fine. Or we could have a beer and relax."

"I put some wine in the fridge this morning too. In case you'd like some. I don't know a whole lot about wine so I hope it's okay."

Nash slipped his hand inside Luke's as they walked to the door. By the time Luke turned the glass doorknob, his heart was pounding. They stopped in the kitchen, he poured them each a glass of wine, and they settled onto the couch. Luke sat at the end this time, and Nash leaned against him.

"This was a wonderful day. I enjoyed getting out and working again. The pizza place was pretty decent too." Nash slid downward and rested his head in Luke's lap. "I enjoyed spending time with you."

"Same here. It was really nice to have someone to spend the day with." He ran his fingers through Nash's hair and immediately understood his mistake as his body tingled and his shaft thickened. He tried to twist, hoping to hide his growing problem.

"Don't you dare."

"What?"

"Try to keep me from knowing Junior is happy to see me."

The heat raced across Luke's face again, only this time his response was frustration. "Dammit! The last time I blushed this much I was in junior high and couldn't keep from getting hard in the locker room."

Nash chuckled. "Yeah, twelve-year-old me had to stop being on the wrestling team because I kept getting a boner."

"Compression shorts. They were what kept me on the team. That and the fact that most of the guys didn't do a thing for me. It was those few I thought were hot that caused the problems."

Nash chuckled as he wriggled into place on Luke's lap. "I was too embarrassed to even ask for a jock. The funny thing is, now that's about all I wear, when I wear anything." With a mischievous glance, he caught Luke's gaze. "Want to see?"

This time Luke smiled back and nodded. "Sure, let's see what ya got."

Nash stood and unbuttoned his pants. He peeled one side back slowly and revealed the familiar wide waistband. Then it hit Luke, and he was torn between giggling and jumping Nash to screw like rabbits. Nash's jock was camouflage. He turned and slipped the pants lower, exposing his bare butt and the twin straps that framed each beautiful cheek.

Without thinking, he leaned forward and caressed Nash's ass with the tips of his fingers. The contact brought a groan from each of them.

"Those are so hot."

"I thought you might like them, after what you told me."

Luke slipped his finger under the strap running over Nash's smooth buttcheek and snapped it. As he did, he realized what Nash said. "So the camo trooper pants, the snug shirt and…." He motioned at Nash's jock. "Are you trying to seduce me?"

"And if I was?"

Luke uncurled from the couch and held out his hand. "Then I'd say let's try the bed."

NASH'S HEART raced as they walked into Luke's bedroom. It dripped masculinity, from the dark wood of the massive four-post bed with its bedding in deep earth tones to the pine floors and dark curtains. It also was filled with Luke's distinctive musk running straight to Nash's cock. It was sex; he'd done this plenty of times over the last ten years. Why did this feel like a first date with a high school sweetheart? Nash chided himself for being so emotional about it. *I've been with other cute guys. It's not a big deal.* But Nash couldn't keep the tension from his body.

"You okay? I thought…."

Nash leaned in and kissed Luke. "Everything's fine. I'm just…." Nash chuckled. "I guess I'm nervous. Stupid, huh?"

Luke exhaled in a gust. "No, I'm nervous as a long-tailed cat in a room full of rockers. Normally I don't give a shit. But around you, I'm so worried I'm going to screw up."

He squeezed Luke's hand and pulled them together, concerned at the depth of his feelings over the tender moment. "You need to stop worrying. I'm a sure thing, so relax."

Luke ran his fingertips over Nash's face, and he shivered. "What does that mean? I keep wondering why a cute guy from Atlanta would want to come all the way out here to see me."

Nash grimaced at his gaffe. He wasn't ready for the fun to end yet. "I'm just saying you don't know how hot you are. Bobby Joe numb nuts was stupid."

"He has kids. I get it. I'm just—"

Nash put his hand over Luke's mouth, his heart breaking at the direction of the conversation. "Sorry I brought him up. My bad. But don't you dare decide you're less important."

Luke's face contorted and his body went rigid.

Nash reached up and caressed his cheek. "Please, promise me."

His body stayed tense in Nash's arms before he relaxed. "Okay, I promise. At least I'll try. I'm sure you didn't come all this way to hear my problems."

He trailed his hand over Luke's chest and slipped the tips of his fingers into the top of his jeans. "I'll listen to whatever you want to tell me. But you can't be the bad guy anymore."

Luke pulled them tight against each other and kissed Nash. The tender kiss grew in heat as Luke ran his tongue over Nash's lips. The fire washed over him, and his shaft stiffened in response. Luke's tongue probed Nash's mouth, but then hesitated. He clasped his hands around Luke's head and returned the kiss with all the passion he could muster.

His tongue plunged in and dueled with Luke's. He probed, kissing harder until his crotch ached. He pressed his hands against Luke's back, enjoying the taut muscles and finally cupping his muscular butt cheeks. As their crotches ground against each other, he sensed Luke pull away. He released him from the kiss but still held tight.

102

"You okay?"

"Too close. Gotta stop or we'll be done."

Nash chuckled as he rubbed his knuckles over the hard nipples outlined against Luke's shirt. Luke sighed and pressed toward Nash. "Not fair. You're making me even hotter."

"Oh? Let's see how you like this." Nash slipped Luke's shirt over his head and tossed it aside. He ran his fingers along Luke's sides and his bulging arms before leaning in to kiss the center of his chest. Then he dove for Luke's nipple. He flicked his tongue over the brown hardness while the sounds coming from Luke grew in volume.

"Ah, crap. That feels good."

Nash rubbed his thumb over the stiff bit of flesh before moving to the other side. He ran his tongue over the second nipple and bit down. Luke sucked in air as he yanked Nash tight against him. His body arched and his muscles tensed in Nash's hands. Luke's enthusiastic response had its own effect on Nash, who fought to keep his body in check. He loved the texture of Luke's chest under his touch and needed more. But before he could act on his desires, two strong hands wrapped around his waist. He lost himself in Luke's hungry brown eyes when he glanced up.

"I think it's my turn."

Luke lifted Nash and easily tossed him onto the bed. He crawled beside Nash and stripped him of his shirt. Leaning over Nash's lean body, he pressed his mouth against one of Nash's small pink nipples before tugging on the rings that ran through each of them. When Luke touched his tongue against Nash, Nash jumped as if electricity shot through his body. He lost himself in the delicious pleasure as Luke worked on first one nipple, then the other. When he reached down and squeezed Nash's crotch, Nash almost lost his load.

"Oh, fuck!"

He grabbed Nash's nipple and twisted it, bringing another loud moan. He flipped over and glared at Luke. "Fuck me. Oh holy hell, fuck me."

He caressed Nash's butt and had him swimming with euphoria. But after a few moments, Nash knew something was wrong. He turned to his side and met Luke's gaze. "What's the deal? You went from full speed to stop in two seconds."

"I guess I did. It was just...."

"What? Spit it out, cowboy."

"Well, I was sorta hoping to bottom for you."

"Really? You sure?"

Luke chuckled as he traced his finger along the bulge formed by Nash's dick. "Hell no I'm not sure. I'm afraid it's going to hurt like hell. I'm worried...."

Nash rolled his eyes. "If you're giving me some Luke butt, it'll be good. Trust me. But now, what do you want to do?"

Luke hesitated. "What if we do both?"

"Both would be amazing." Nash considered Luke. "I think you should go first. Being really horny helps cover up a lot of being uncomfortable."

"What about you, you know, with my guy?" Luke motioned at his straining shaft.

"It's fine. I'm a professional." There was a heartbeat of a pause as Nash tried to cover the slip. "Compared to you."

"You've got me there, since I've never done this before."

Nash curled up until he sat in front of Luke. He opened Luke's jeans to find a pair of skintight compression shorts. The sheer fabric left little to the imagination, but amped up Nash's desire to breed this hot man. He leaned forward and licked through the fabric along Luke's hard length. He pushed Luke onto the bed and tugged his jeans off. Nash kissed the wet spot marking the tip of Luke's shaft before peeling off the shorts to expose Luke's handsome body, his cock angling to one side.

He glanced at Luke. "How close are you?"

"I'm about to go off like fireworks on the Fourth."

Nash snickered and slapped Luke on the hip. "Roll over and I'll show you my favorite thing, even more than sucking your pits."

Luke rolled over slowly, watching Nash the entire time. He grinned and slapped Luke's buttcheeks again. This time a small groan escaped his lips. It wasn't long before Luke's chest pressed against the bed and Nash lay between Luke's legs.

He trembled when Nash grabbed his asscheeks and squeezed them tight. Nash's tongue touched on the patch of skin under Luke's nuts and lapped slowly upward. He squirmed under him, his moans filling the room.

"Fuck. It feels good when you do that."

"You like it?"

"Like it? I love it! Oh, yeah."

"Good, 'cause rimming you is my favorite fantasy."

"Get busy, then. 'Cause this is amazing."

He pried Luke's butt open, licking and teasing his way lower until he found the opening. He flicked his tongue over the dusky skin until it was coated with spit. Once he'd accomplished that, he wriggled his tongue deeper inside.

The minutes slipped past as each man lost himself in the pleasure that filled him. Nash pulled back, to Luke's disappointed groan. "Ah, shit. Don't stop."

"Calm down, stud. I just need some lube." He grabbed the bottle from the side table and clicked it open to run a stream where it was needed. As he spread it over the puckered opening, Luke grabbed the edge of the bed and arched his back. His body shook as Nash pressed the tip of his finger inside. By the time it sank to the first knuckle, Luke was bucking up to meet his exploration.

"Shit, holy freaking shit. Put it in already," Luke said.

"Hang on. We're just getting started." Nash slipped out and squirted more lube on his fingers. He lay beside Luke, caressing his body as he worked to open him for what was coming. Nash decided he was ready when Luke was reduced to a chorus of moans and his body glistened with a fine sheen of sweat.

"Where's the condoms?"

Luke weakly motioned to his dresser. "There. Top drawer, left."

Nash bounded off the bed, his cock so hard that it hovered in front of his stomach. After finding what he needed, he moved between Luke's thick thighs. He rolled on a condom and slathered it with lube.

He pressed the tip of his cock against Luke's opening and slipped inside while he gauged Luke's reaction. He pushed farther until Luke tensed, then paused and ran his hands over Luke's back until it relaxed him and he sank back into the bed.

"You okay?"

"I've never felt anything that good. It was like lightning hit my dick."

Nash pressed inward while he leaned down and kissed along Luke's ear. The moans and sighs from both of them filled the room. But as Nash reached bottom, Luke seized under him.

"Stop!"

"What's wrong?"

"Just stop. You hit it. I about lost it."

Nash chuckled softly. "It does feel pretty amazing, doesn't it? The bend in my cock makes it easy to hit your prostate."

"I don't know what it was, but I was about to shoot."

He nibbled on the side of Luke's neck until he squirmed. Then Nash pressed in slowly, rewarded by a gasp from Luke as he ground his crotch against the muscular man's ass. He wrapped his arms around Luke's thick chest and tugged on his nipples as he eased out.

"I've never felt this before. Never. You're right. You're a pro."

Nash froze, but then refocused on the man under him. "Good. I'm glad you like it. Because you're so tight, I'm not going to last much longer."

Luke simply moaned and pressed himself backward as Nash pushed toward him. Their movements became synchronized as the room once again filled with moans and sighs. The scent of men in heat assaulted Nash's senses. He moved faster until he was slamming into Luke. The hot cowboy grabbed the bedding in both fists, his eyes closed as Nash thundered toward a climax. He clamped his hands on Luke's shoulders as he pounded the muscular butt in front of him. Then a familiar sensation began and Nash hit a new level of pleasure.

Lost in the ecstasy, Nash jerked and moaned, gliding his hands over Luke's sweaty skin. The waves of pleasure went on and on, but with a final tightening, Nash's orgasm ended. He lay across Luke, gasping for air as he drifted back to reality.

He moved higher and Luke tilted his head. Their lips met in a soft kiss. They kissed again and again until Nash softened and slipped from inside Luke.

"Your turn, stud."

Luke chuckled. "I don't know that I'll last long enough to even touch you."

"Roll on your back."

Luke eased into place, his cock standing at attention. Nash put a drop of lube on the deep red crown, unrolled the condom over Luke's shaft, and smeared it with the gel. He struggled for a moment before he smirked. "Dude, Magnum, you need Magnum."

Luke looked at him blankly, and then his face became a deep shade of crimson. But before he could reply, Nash straddled him and ground his ass against Luke, trapping his cock in the cleft of his ass. Luke laced his fingers together behind his head, a look of sheer pleasure covering his face. Luke's musky pit smell washed over Nash again and again. His body responded and soon his cock was again hard as steel and hovering against his stomach.

He leaned forward, bracing himself on Luke, reached between them and wrapped his hand around Luke's cock. He rubbed it over his entrance a few times, letting it dip deeper with each pass. He wedged himself against it and slowly sank downward. Having taken Luke's shaft without too much trouble before, he expected to take it easily. But Luke stretched him as he'd experienced only a few times. He was beginning to think he would have to try something else when Luke slipped inside.

He gasped through the swirl of ecstasy and pain. But in seconds, the pain subsided and he pressed downward again. This time he moved without stopping until he had taken Luke's entire shaft. His eyes fluttered shut as he ground his hips against Luke, hitting his sweet spot each time.

His eyes flew open at Luke's touch. The tug of his fingers on the rings through Nash's nipples intensified the sensations until he knew he was building for round two. Soon the two of them were moving in unison, and Nash knew neither of them was far from reaching their climax. Their bodies pounded together, Luke ramming hard inside him each time Nash slammed down. He grabbed Luke's nipples and rolled them between his fingers.

Luke growled, grabbed Nash's hips, and fucked him as fast as he could move. Nash heard a cry of pleasure filling the room and realized it was him. As Luke pummeled him again and again, he knew it was happening. He was going to come again from Luke's fucking.

As the first strand shot from his cock, Luke pinned them together and trembled. Their twin orgasms were one of the most powerful feelings Nash had ever experienced. As Luke's growl echoed through the room, the muscular body under Nash shook. He gyrated his hips slowly, enjoying the full sensation until Luke pulled him down for a kiss. Nash relished the scents and tastes of sex that surrounded them, enjoying the moment with Luke and trying not to think beyond right now.

Luke's strong hands cradled his head as they gasped for air. He pulled their foreheads together as they shared deep emotions that Nash refused to label. They lay together until Luke softened and slipped out. Nash kissed his forehead and then crawled off. He knew Luke was watching him intently as he stepped into the bathroom. He cleaned himself before coming back to stand over Luke and grin. "I seem to have made a mess."

Luke returned the unrepentant expression. "I kinda like it...."

The simple declaration shook Nash more than he thought it should. But he reached down with the wet cloth he'd brought and cleaned Luke, including taking care of the almost overflowing condom. He sat on the side of the bed and ran his hand down Luke's side. "Did you want to cuddle?"

Luke flipped back the sheet he'd pulled over his naked body. "Get in here."

A smile covered Nash's face as he crawled into bed with Luke and kissed him softly. "That was amazing. It really was."

"Same here. I've never felt that good."

They lay touching and kissing, reveling in the afterglow until the room was dark. Nash sighed and pushed himself off the bed. "I guess I should get in my bed."

Luke slid his hand down Nash's arm and closed it around his wrist. "Do you have to?"

Nash turned back and his resolve melted as he fell into Luke's deep brown eyes. "You want me to stay?"

"Yes, I do."

Nash crawled into bed and nestled into Luke's arms. He turned so they were facing each other and ran the tips of his fingers over Luke's body. Little by little his eyelids got heavier until he fell asleep nestled in Luke's embrace.

CHAPTER NINE

NASH'S EYES flew open at a kiss on the back of his neck. The next thing that registered was the warm body behind him. Nash didn't wake up in other men's beds. He didn't let that happen. But as he got a second soft kiss, he knew he'd broken another of his rules.

"Morning, sunshine. About time you crawled outta them tall weeds."

Nash chuckled as he squirmed back against Luke. "You're going to use up all these folksy sayings one day."

"Oh, that was how my granddad woke me every morning. I guess that's the first time I've used it since they passed."

"Why? It's kind of cute."

"I haven't woke up with anyone since then."

The admission tugged at Nash's heart. He pulled Luke's arm over him, enjoying the scents that filled the air blowing around them as the sheet settled. Nash started rubbing his hands over Luke's arm. He tugged them together and kissed the back of Nash's neck again. "As much as I'd like to play around, Chris will be here soon. As sure as we start something, she'll show up early."

Nash twisted until they faced each other and kissed the middle of Luke's throat. As he reached his chest, Luke sighed. "You're a bad influence. You make me wish she wasn't coming."

Nash chuckled and pulled away, swinging his legs over the edge of the bed to lay back and resting his head on Luke's stomach. It was one of the most peaceful times Nash could remember. He turned his head slowly and kissed the tip of Luke's morning wood.

"Okay, I'm not going to be able to keep saying no. And besides, I gotta pee like a Russian race horse."

Nash chuckled as his head bounced against the bed when Luke rolled from under him. He sat up and watched Luke trot to the

110

bathroom. A familiar sound filled the room, and Nash laughed at Luke's sigh of relief.

Luke leaned back and grinned at Nash. "You know you'll sound just like that when you get rid of yours."

"Yeah, I hate to tell you but I'm one of those people who are up and down all night taking a leak. So it's not usually too impressive."

Luke shook off the last drops and flushed before turning on the shower. Nash sat on the bed and enjoyed the show as Luke climbed in and lathered his body. It didn't take long before he was rinsing off. Once the last of the white foam was gone, he turned off the water, slipped out, dried off, and wrapped the towel around his waist. At that point, Nash knew the show was over for now.

Nash pushed himself off the bed and made his way into the bathroom. He swatted Luke's butt as he made his way to the toilet.

"Hey! Careful. Something got poked up there and it's a little sore."

Nash tugged the towel and let it drop to the floor. He ran the palm of his hand over Luke's butt. "Poor baby. We won't do that nasty old fucking anymore."

Luke twisted and kissed Nash. "Like hell we won't. But I don't want to hear any giggles if I'm sitting funny on the horse today."

Nash ran his hands down Luke's torso and squeezed his heavy cock. "I promise. No giggles."

Luke shoved him toward the shower. "Get cleaned up. Chris doesn't like to wait."

Several minutes later found the pair sitting at the kitchen table downing toast and coffee. Luke was eating a piece as the door burst open.

"Come on, slugs! Get your happy asses up. I'm ready to rope."

"You know, one of these days you're going to walk in on something you didn't want to see with that darn key."

Chris grabbed a piece of toast, smeared it with jam, and began eating. She glanced at Luke and froze, staring at him. Then she turned to scrutinize Nash.

"Well damn! You got laid."

Luke's face turned bright red, and Nash was shocked to feel heat rise on his skin too. "Chris! Knock it off. How many times have I told you to not worry about my sex life?"

"About a million. But this time you actually have one."

Nash was surprised when Chris winked at him and walked out chuckling. Once she closed the door, he turned to Luke.

"Sorry. She loves to embarrass me," Luke said.

Nash tried to hide his reaction. That was the first time in a long time he'd been embarrassed. "She did a heck of a job... on both of us."

Luke inhaled through his nose and slowly released it. "She's stuck with me through a lot of stuff. I'm willing to cut her some slack."

They heard the horses as the door to Chris's trailer swung open. Luke pushed back from the table. "We better go. It sounds like she is even more impatient than usual."

THE MORNING had left Luke rattled. He wasn't sure how to feel. Sometimes he wanted to use duct tape on Chris's mouth, and this was one of those times. She was backing her gelding out of the trailer by the time he and Nash made their way to the arena. He pushed open the gate for Chris and walked across the loose dirt. About that time, he realized Nash probably had no idea what they were about to do. He motioned Nash closer.

"We need to work the calves in this pen into the chute. Then I'll go saddle my horse."

Nash watched the multicolored calves walk in front of them. "Just put them in the chute? I can do that. Go get saddled up."

Luke started to argue but realized if Nash had trouble they'd get it straightened out later. "Sounds good. I'll be back in a second."

He waited to make sure Nash wasn't going to have any trouble. When he saw Nash had the situation well in hand, he headed at a trot to saddle his horse. He was cinching the final strap when he noticed Chris sitting on her horse, staring over the fences in Nash's direction.

"He is kind of hot, even with all the metal."

"There's more metal than you can see."

Chris shook her head. "My boy has more kinks than I thought."

Luke looked around the horse at Chris. "Don't run him off. I kinda like him."

"Okay, but I'm not going to stand around and let another Bobby happen. But from the grin you've been wearing since I got here, I'd guess he's already outdone Bobby in one important area."

In one smooth motion, Luke vaulted into the saddle. He smiled at Chris, then reined his horse toward the arena, and his smile seemed permanently etched on his face as Chris eased alongside him.

"Yeah, that's the smile of a satisfied man. No question about that."

"Hush."

"For now." Chris kicked her horse into a gallop and her laughter drifted to Luke. But he didn't care how much Chris teased him, he was going to savor last night. He leaned forward, clicked his tongue, and shot after Chris.

Once they were inside, Luke made his way to the corral where Nash had successfully penned the handful of calves. He threw his leg over the saddle and lowered himself to the ground. He walked over and opened the chute gate.

"Press them a little tighter. You can use the white gates."

Nash waved his arms, and the calves surged away from him and directly to where Luke wanted them. Luke was back on horseback and in the box. He situated his horse in the exact spot where he wanted it, and signaled Nash.

The spring-loaded gate shot open and a calf bolted from the chute. A second later its headlong plunge snapped the barrier open as Luke raced after it. The lariat circled above his head and shot out after the calf like a striking snake. Luke loved the familiar sensations as the rope settled around the calf's head and the horse dropped his hindquarters to stop it.

Luke flung himself off the horse and was at the end of the rope in a heartbeat. He flipped the calf, grabbed his piggin string, and tied the legs. The instant he finished, both hands went into the air.

"Damn! That was amazing. Your fucking horse practically sat down," Nash said.

Chris looked at the stopwatch. "Not bad for an old man."

"Oh, really? You want to make this interesting? Loser buys lunch."

"You're on, big boy. I'm going to whip your ass from here to Poteau."

Luke swung back into the saddle, eased his horse forward a few steps to take the tension off the rope, and turned to Nash. "You mind letting him go?"

Nash trotted to the calf, loosened the rope, and slipped it over its head. It took a few seconds, but soon the calf was untied. It jumped to its feet and ran a few yards before slowing to a walk.

Luke coiled his lariat and looped it over the saddle horn. He grinned down at Nash. "Wanna run and see if I can catch you?"

Nash cocked his eyebrow. "Oh yeah, that would be so fair. Chasing me down using a horse."

"Don't knock it. You might like it all tied up," Chris said as she trotted her horse beside them.

Nash retorted, "It's extra."

"Woohoo! What's the value pack?"

Luke didn't like the direction the teasing was taking this time. Something about the tone coming from Nash was knotting Luke's insides. "All right, ladies. We going to stand around chitchatting or am I gonna win a free lunch?"

"First, thanks for recognizing the lady that I am. Second, bring it on. I'm gonna whip your ass," Chris said.

"Get your dang horse in the box."

Chris backed her horse in, grabbed the piggin string between her teeth, and adjusted the size of her loop until she was satisfied. Nash reset the barrier while she got settled. She glanced over to find Nash's gaze locked on her. She nodded and he released the calf. Luke held the stopwatch tight as his friend flew down the rope and tossed the animal. A second later, she threw her hands into the air.

"Done! Suck it, cowboy."

Luke glanced down at the timer. "A little over eight. Not bad."

"Not bad? Bullshit. I should've bet you more 'cause this is gonna be a slaughter."

They dropped into a rhythm, and before Luke realized how much time had passed, they had put the calves through twice and he was getting tired. He looked at the times he'd been recording and turned to Chris. "Looks like this calf will be the tiebreaker."

Nash loaded the steer into the chute and reset the barrier. A few seconds later, Luke was chasing the animal across the arena. He flipped the noose in front of him and was off the horse before the calf hit the end of the rope. Every step went as smooth as possible, and he soon flung his hands into the air.

"Damn! Seven nine. Not bad, Meyers. Not bad at all."

They handed off the stopwatch. Chris moved into position and was off after the calf like a shot. Without a missed step, she chased him down and seconds later had the calf's feet flying through the air. Her hand circled around the calf's legs and shot upward.

She spun toward Luke with a look of triumph. "That's it! Beat your ass, didn't I?"

Luke looked down as the calf bawled once, then kicked its legs free. "Doesn't matter. Your calf didn't make the six seconds for its feet to stay tied. Lunch will be so sweet."

Chris spun in time to see the calf run toward the others, and turned to Luke. "Fine. Asshole. My time was better."

Luke shook his head and rubbed his hands together. "Something delicious and expensive. Hmm. Oh yeah."

"You butt. Let's get the horses unsaddled. I'm picking lunch. Nothing said I had to eat the crap you like."

Luke chuckled as he opened the gate to allow the calves back together. He waited until Chris disappeared into the barn before grinning at Nash. "She always gets in too big of a hurry on the tie offs when she's under pressure. I knew we were getting a free meal."

Nash stayed beside Luke as they walked the calves back to the grass-filled pen. Nash glanced over. "You looked good, really good. You're both so fast."

Luke glanced at Nash to see if he was joking, but his expression was serious. He considered the statement before replying to Nash. "I'm good enough for the local circuit, but the pros are at least a second or two faster than me. I know that doesn't sound like much, but it would take a lot of practice and I still might never get to their level. I don't have that kind of time. I have to keep the ranch going."

They walked a few steps farther before either spoke again. "Doesn't that bum you out when you can't do your dream thing?" Nash asked.

Luke thought about the question for several seconds. "No, not really. It's not that big of a deal to me. I think I'm not as competitive as some of the guys. Don't get me wrong, I like to win. But my world doesn't end if someone beats me at roping a calf."

They walked in silence to the gate. Nash stayed behind the calves while Luke eased in front of them and let them in. The calves were well aware of what was on the other side and rushed past Luke. He enjoyed the scene as the animals walked from clump to clump selecting only the choicest bites. He sensed Nash drawing up beside him.

"Anything else they need?" Nash asked.

"Nope, their water trough was full. They'll eat grass until they can't hold any more, then find a shady spot to lay down."

"Sounds like they have a pretty sweet setup around here."

"They have it good for a while. But they get too big. When that happens, I sell them and buy some more."

Nash nodded and began the trip back to the barn. Luke stood looking at him, then trotted to catch up. They took a few steps before Luke couldn't stand not knowing. "You didn't have much to say."

Nash glanced at him and shrugged. "Nothing much to ask. They get too big and you take them to the sale barn. They're steers. What else are you going to do with them?"

Luke came to an abrupt halt and stared at Nash.

"What?" Nash asked.

"I keep forgetting that you grew up on a farm and not in Atlanta."

"Yeah, it was a little place, nothing they could make a living from."

"Do you miss it?"

"Maybe. I don't know. I always liked the animals. All of the livestock you have remind me of them. But I haven't talked to anyone from Ozark in years."

Luke considered asking more questions but saw how tense Nash had become. He held his tongue on the remainder of the short walk. They came in to find Chris had taken care of Luke's horse and already had hers in the trailer.

"Typical men, stroll up just as the woman finishes doing the work."

"I could have taken care of my own horse, Chris."

There was a moment of tension, and she broke into a smile. "I'm yankin' your chain. I'll get mine taken care of while you two clean up, then you can swing by and pick me up."

"Okay, see you in a few minutes."

He and Nash watched as Chris pulled out of the driveway. Once she'd disappeared behind the trees, Luke grinned at Nash. "We better go change clothes. She'll be cranky if we make her wait."

Nash hesitated.

"Something wrong?"

"I was going to borrow your washer today. I need to wash some clothes."

"I can loan you some. Like we did for the swimsuit."

"Luke, even if they didn't fall off my ass, they'd be way too short."

"Let me check. I think I have a pair of new Wranglers that might work. One of my aunts sent them to me last year for Christmas. She apparently thinks I'm six-two and have about a twenty-eight-inch waist."

Nash chuckled and shook his head. "Has she not seen you since you were twelve?"

"No, that's just it. She sees me every year at the family reunion. Of course, she never remembers my name. That might be part of the problem."

"Well, if they fit then that's fine. Otherwise I can relax and watch TV." Nash tensed and caught Luke's gaze. "Unless you don't want me in the house alone. I would totally understand. I could snooze on the porch or something."

"No, no. I don't care if you stay here. There's nothing to steal in that old house anyway. It's just...."

A few seconds ticked by until Nash prompted him. "Just what?"

"Just that I wanted everyone to see the handsome guy who's staying with me. Sorry."

"And if we happened to run into Bobby again?"

"And show the twerp how happy I am? I wouldn't be offended."

Nash chuckled and pushed Luke to the house. "You better hope these jeans your aunt sent fit me better than the swimsuit or nobody's going to be impressed."

NASH WALKED a step in front of Luke but could feel his stare following him. They'd almost reached the entrance to the cafe when Chris piped up.

"If you're going to jump his bones, you shouldn't have brought me. Although I can't really blame you. That's one cute butt."

Heat traveled up Nash's neck and across his face as Chris managed to embarrass both of them again.

"Chris!"

"Hey, I'm not the one with their eyes locked on his goods since you got to my house."

"Oh my God! Shut up."

Chris grinned and held the door. "I'll teach you to bet with me."

They slipped inside and the waitress waved and motioned them to an empty table. The burgundy vinyl crackled as they scooted across. Luke gave the menus she'd given each of them a cursory glance before tossing it to the table as Nash slipped in beside him.

"I know what I want," Luke said.

Chris gave him a dismissive wave. "You always get the same thing. Give the rest of us some time."

Nash glanced to Luke. "What's so good that you always get the same thing?"

"Homemade biscuits and sausage gravy. It's amazing."

Nash chuckled and patted Luke's thigh. "You and your biscuits. It's not even breakfast."

"Biscuits aren't just for breakfast anymore," Luke quipped.

The waitress appeared and took their orders with practiced efficiency. Soon the table was filled with plates of food. They shared dishes until almost everything was eaten. Nash hadn't realized how hungry a morning of helping with the roping left him. They were down to the last of their vanilla malts when Luke scooted out of the booth.

"Be right back."

Nash riveted his gaze on Luke's backside as he wound his way across the crowded diner.

"When are you going to tell him?"

He reclined against the booth, fighting to relax. He met eyes with Chris, knowing where this was going but not willing to be the one to say it. "What are you talking about?"

"Your web page is pretty… interesting."

"How did you find out?"

"Well, a couple of your comments made me wonder. And Nash Gallo in Atlanta narrows it down. I'm surprised you used your real name on the site."

"That's what happens when an eighteen-year-old fills out those damn forms."

"So when are you going to tell him? 'Cause I know you haven't."

"It's gotten complicated…."

Chris's glance flicked across the cafe before coming back to Nash. "Luke is a really sweet guy and has had enough assholes in his life. You hurt him, and I'll cut your nuts off."

Nash lifted his eyebrows and set his mouth. "Luke is a nice guy. I'm not trying to hurt him. I don't know how he's going to take the news. I hate to ruin everything."

"Last time he was Bobby's secret and even though he should have known better, it about killed him. Don't keep more secrets from him."

The jangle of spurs coming closer marked Luke's return. They both glanced up at him as he slid into the seat beside Nash. "So what's going on? You both look like lunch didn't settle very well."

"No, nothing like that. Just chatting," Nash said.

Luke looked from one to the other of them but didn't press the question. A few seconds later, Chris emptied her shake and banged the glass to the table. "Well, I got more things to do than sit around the cafe and drink coffee. I'm several decades away from that being my day."

Before long they were dropping Chris off at her ranch and making their way back home. They parked in front of the house, but Luke made no motion to get out of the pickup. As the silence stretched out Luke glanced at Nash. "I hope Chris didn't piss you off. She's kind of protective of me. And I guess I am of her too. We've been friends for as long as I could remember." He chuckled a little. "She's even how I knew I was gay. She offered to show me her parts, and I wasn't interested."

Nash laughed. "That would be a clue."

"Yeah, it was an eye opener. Thank God she never got her pants open."

Nash said, "So I guess you're more toward the six side of the scale."

"Oh yeah, I don't like fish at all. I'm beef one-hundred percent of the time." Luke's expression sobered. "I didn't want Chris to run you off."

"She didn't. I get that she doesn't want you hurt."

Luke shook his head, his expression hardening. "I'm not a kid, and she and I are the same age anyway. I don't need her to defend me."

Nash shrugged. "Don't sweat it. It must be nice to have someone who'll be there whenever you need them."

"It isn't going to change so I guess I'll stop worrying about it." He glanced at Nash. "I was going to go look at a new herd bull this guy I know has. Did you want to go? If you don't, that's cool. You're welcome to chill out here."

"Nah, I'll go. There's nothing I like to see better than a swinging set of nuts. And since you're busy...." Nash leered at Luke, who turned deep red.

He stammered a few times before giving up, putting the truck in gear, and heading toward the highway. They rode without speaking until Nash glanced at Luke. "I didn't mean to embarrass you. I thought you liked the teasing before."

Luke stiffened again, then deflated like a cheap inner tube. "I guess I don't know how to take it."

"You're cute and hung. Nothing I say would ever be bad."

"See? I know I'm short. Hung isn't necessarily a plus either."

"Well, I like guys who are muscular, and I think you're a great height. As for your endowment...." Nash slipped his hand into Luke's lap and squeezed his package. "I think you've got the perfect equipment."

Luke shook his head but stayed relaxed. "Okay, enough of that junk. What do you want to do? There's only a few more days before you have to go back to Atlanta and.... Never mind, I don't want to mess up the moment."

A quiver rolled through Nash. "What? You can't start and chicken shit out."

"I was going to say that we'll be back to talking over the computer and texting. I'm kinda bummed out about that."

Nash's heart constricted at the thought. "Yeah, I'm not really looking forward to that either. Let's just enjoy each other. You never know what's going to happen."

Luke fell silent and Nash was left to his own thoughts. *She's right. I have to tell him.* Nash turned to stare out the window. Lost in thought as another dream fell apart. He hardened himself and decided he was going to enjoy what he could.

After checking on the livestock, they started down the road to the friend of Luke's. Nash wasn't very talkative so most of the trip was uneventful. He stirred back to his surroundings when the truck slowed.

"We're here."

Nash was startled as they pulled up to the upscale house with what seemed to be miles of white board fences. He tried to take it all in as they drove up the winding driveway.

"Some doctor from Fort Smith owns it. But they're almost never here. They raise a few horses. But when they bought the place, they bought the Brangus herd too. They've got one of the best in this part of the state."

"Isn't all this stuff expensive?"

"Oh yeah, expensive as hell. But when they come out, they want it to be pretty. So the ranch manager keeps it pretty."

Nash sat quietly as they pulled up to a tall metal corral. By the time they climbed out of the pickup, someone was coming across the gravel to meet them. Nash studied his muscular body and the rough scruff that covered his face. He bristled as Luke shook hands with the guy. Jealousy reared its head and sank its teeth into Nash.

"Hey, Luke. How's things going?"

"Not bad, not bad at all. And yourself?"

"Fair to middling. It's getting pretty dry. Makes me nervous that we might be hit with more brush fires."

"Oh, I know. My place is a kindling box waiting for a match. But they're forecasting rain next week. So we can hope."

"Yup, hope. That's what we live on round here. But you didn't drive all this way to jaw with me. I think you'll like this bull. He's tame as a kitten and heavily muscled."

The three of them threaded their way through a small gate that snapped shut behind them. Nash couldn't avoid seeing the bull, but its reaction made his stomach flip-flop. It had been grazing, but the instant they moved closer, its head snapped upward, its ears cocked forward, and it snorted at them. Nash had to admit, it was one of the biggest animals he'd ever seen. Its muscles rippled and bulged under its black coat.

"Nice bull, he seems a little on edge, though," Luke said.

"Nah, he's calm as they come."

At that moment, the bull pawed the ground, threw a spire of dust into the air, and ran a few feet closer before stopping his charge.

Nash looked first at one of them, then the other. "You guys can stand here and talk about Junior, but I think I'll wait on the other side of the fence."

Luke grinned at him before turning back to discuss the bull. Nash slipped through the gate and stood watching the two talk about the merits of the candidate for Luke's new herd sire. As the time stretched out, Nash decided this wasn't going to happen soon. He sat in the slight shade of the fence, idly drawing patterns in the dust. He lost himself in the designs he'd been toying with for an addition to the tattoo that wound its way down his left side. He became so submerged in his work that it took him longer than normal to realize something was making a whining noise.

He stood, looking for the source of the pitiful sound. His search resulted in the discovery of a half-grown puppy locked in one of the stalls. It looked at him and made one of the most pathetic sounds Nash had ever heard, then barked. He worked his way into the stall and held out a hand. The puppy dragged itself forward, stretched out its neck, and sniffed at the tips of Nash's fingers.

"Hey, boy. What's wrong with you? Can you not walk?"

Nash eased his fingers over the dog's head and gently rubbed between his ears. After a few seconds, the puppy wheezed and laid his head on the floor of the stall. He gave the pup a few minutes as he rubbed its back and hind leg.

"What'cha got?"

Nash glanced up to find Luke and the ranch manager looking at him over the stall door. "Sorry, I kept hearing him whine."

"It's okay. I don't know what I'm going to do with him. I've had him for a month or so but he's so excited by the cattle. I always lock him up when I'm working the cows. Somehow he got out. One of them nailed him. The vet did an X-ray and said he couldn't find anything, but he seems to be getting weaker and weaker, and he can barely walk with that bum back leg."

"What're you going to do with him?" Nash asked.

"I don't know what to do. I'm worried he's not going to make it. It'd be a shame too. He's going to be a beautiful blue-merle border collie."

Luke walked inside, squatted beside Nash, and reached over to pet him. He jerked his hand back when the puppy growled.

Nash chuckled. "Relax, it's just a puppy. He won't hurt you."

"Dogs don't seem to care much for me. I don't know what it is. They've never liked me. One bit me when I was little. I still have the scar."

Nash reached over and ruffled his white ears. "Oh, he's seeing who he can get his bluff in with. Border collies are kind of fussy that way."

Luke relaxed but kept his distance. After another round of petting, Nash reluctantly stood to leave. But he'd taken no more than a couple of steps before the puppy barked and began whimpering. Nash looked back to see the pup trying to follow him, dragging one of his legs.

"He likes you. He never does that for me."

Nash looked up at the ranch manager, close to bursting into tears. "What?"

"Y'all should take him home with you. I'm afraid he's going to die on me."

Nash's heart ached at the big blue eyes looking up at him. There was a catch in his throat as he wiped his face. "Can't. I'm only here for a couple more days."

Tense silence filled the space until Luke sighed. "You can nurse him back to health while you're here. I'm sure someone will take him once he's well."

"Luke? You sure?"

"Yeah, what the heck. We didn't have any plans for the rest of your stay, so we can hang around the house if you want."

Nash threw his arms around Luke in a huge hug, then scooped the dog up in his arms. His smile was so wide his jaws hurt. The dog looked at him with his ears folded back against his head and sniffed Nash.

"I think he likes you," Luke said and turned toward the pickup. A strange sense of warmth filled Nash as he settled the puppy onto the floor between his feet. Luke climbed in on the other side, and Nash stared at him for quite some time before Luke met his eyes.

"What?"

"We need to go by the pet store and get a few things."

Silence filled the cab for several miles when Luke shook his head. "Why do I think this is going to become an expensive free dog?"

LUKE CARRIED the dog bed in one hand and the bag full of toys and treats in the other. He handed Nash the keys to unlock the door and stood looking around the room. He still didn't understand what had come over him. He'd avoided dogs like the plague for years. Now he'd let a guy who was visiting for a few days talk him into bringing one home. *It already growled at me. What the heck was I thinking?*

"Where do you think we should put him?"

"The utility room?"

Nash glared at Luke. "He needs to be where we can see him. Now be serious."

I was being serious. "Where would you suggest?"

"Well, like I said, he needs to see us. I guess in the kitchen."

"You're going to have to take him outside constantly. Otherwise…."

"I know, I know. I don't want the house to smell like dog either. Which means the first thing we're doing is a bath."

"At least he shouldn't have fleas. Jeff said he'd given him the heartworm medicine that takes care of that."

"I wish we had something really good to feed him. He looks like he hasn't been eating too well."

Luke considered the puppy as it sagged against Nash. "I have some liver in the freezer from the last calf we had processed. I could defrost it, I guess."

Nash flashed him a smile that melted his insides. "Thank you. I'll go wash him up."

The next hour or so was lost in preparing Luke's house to accommodate a dog. He managed to defrost the liver and only cook a little of it, then chopped it into small chunks. Regardless of Luke's issues with dogs, Nash obviously loved the animal. He was chatting with and kissing the dog while he rubbed him dry. He wrapped the pup in a towel and sat cross-legged with him in his lap. He grinned at Luke.

"Did you get the liver?"

Luke handed him the bowl of diced meat and watched as Nash fed him bit by bit. At first the dog wasn't interested, but after Nash slipped a few bites in, he developed an appetite. Before he stopped eating, the bowl was half-gone, his stomach was distended, and he lay sprawled across Nash's lap. Luke watched while Nash rubbed the pup's stomach.

"He looks pretty comfortable. I guess we need to come up with a name. I can't keep calling him dog or pup," Luke said. At the sound of his voice, the dog opened his eyes and stared at Luke just before a whine came from him.

"Oh jeez, it's not that bad. Mess with me and I'll name you Whiner."

Nash rubbed across the dog's full belly. "I think he's full. Who knew liver was the magic food?"

"Well he can have all he wants. I use it for fishing bait."

Nash eased from the floor and carried the pup to the corner of the kitchen where Luke had put his bed. He sat beside the dog until he fell asleep.

Luke shook his head, conflicted about the addition to his house. He hoped Jeff would take the pup back when he was better. He stared at the scene until Nash uncoiled himself from the floor and walked over to Luke. His resistance melted when Nash draped an arm over his shoulder and gave him a hug.

"He has to be one of the most beautiful dogs I've ever seen. Those eyes are so blue."

Luke leaned into Nash, enjoying the contact. "He is a cute dog, I have to admit."

"Bingo."

"What?"

"Bingo. I think we should call him Bingo."

"Like the song?"

"Yeah, pretty much."

Luke shrugged, still not certain how he felt about the new guest. "Fine with me. I don't think Jeff had really gave him a name yet." He made his way to the fridge and started pulling out food to make sandwiches. He soon had the table covered with various ingredients and a loaf of bread. He found Nash grinning at him.

"What?"

"You really don't like dogs, do you?"

Luke tilted his head and studied the quiet form. "They don't like me. That's all there is to it. But he likes you."

Luke made sandwiches and pulled out a bag of chips to share. Nash moved so he could watch Bingo, but the dog was sound asleep. He took a few bites of his sandwich, then stared at the sleeping puppy again. "Is he still breathing? Should I check on him?"

A sleepy snort came from Bingo and Luke chuckled. "He's fine. Just stuffed with liver until he can't move."

The pair finished the meal and Luke started making them each a float. He glanced up to see Nash watching him. "I guess I didn't ask. Do you want a Coke float?"

"Sure. It's been kind of busy. Maybe we could watch some TV?"

Luke topped off each ice-cream-filled glass with Coke, then handed one to Nash along with a spoon. Soon they were snuggled against each other with the television going. He enjoyed the heat of Nash's body against his, and Nash's scent curled through his nose. The combination spoke to Luke, his jeans clearly showing the results. He curled himself down and kissed the top of Nash's head. Nash twisted in his lap until he was smiling up at Luke.

"What are you doing?" asked Nash.

"Trying to get lucky?"

Nash chuckled. "It wouldn't take much. Like I said before, I'm pretty much a sure thing."

Luke curled down again. The surge of pleasure that washed through him as their lips touched left him panting for air. Lightning crackled through his system when the tip of Nash's tongue traced along his lips.

A whine came from the floor in front of the couch. *What the heck?* Luke broke the kiss and leaned forward to find two ice blue eyes staring up at him.

"Well crap...."

Nash looked and chuckled. "He's hungry, I bet. But he made it all the way in here. He must be better." He rolled off the couch and lifted the dog in his arms.

Luke's shaft throbbed as he watched Nash's tight butt on its way back into the kitchen. *Dang it. Cockblocked by a mutt!*

He sat on the couch, his bulge clearly visible, while Nash repeated the process of feeding the dog. By the time his aching cock went down, Bingo had eaten the liver that was left. Nash glanced over his shoulder at Luke. "Do you have more liver?"

"I do. But let's let it defrost overnight and try some of the treats we bought. Not now, though. I think right now you should take him out to use the bathroom before you have to clean up after him."

"Good plan." Nash scooped up the pup and made his way out the door. Luke began to clean up, and a short time later Nash and Bingo made their way back into the house. "We made it just in time. But he's taken care of peeing and pooping."

"Put him to bed. I'm ready for some sleep." *Or to get in bed anyway.*

Luke stepped beside Nash and interlocked their fingers before he leaned in and kissed Nash. When he did, Bingo whined and then barked.

Nash spun, walked to the dog, and petted him until he settled back into his bed. He turned to look at Luke with a plea in his expression. "He's scared, and it's a new place. Do you think he could sleep beside the bed tonight?"

Luke glanced at the four eyes beseeching him and let out a sigh of resignation. "Okay, but only tonight. He has to learn to sleep by himself."

"Sure, sure. No problem. I'll work with him tomorrow about staying in the kitchen."

"That'd be good. Because I'm just getting used to sharing my bed. I don't think I want to share it with a dog too."

"I'll put his bed where I can reach him. I'm sure he'll be fine after tonight."

Nash arranged Bingo's bed and settled the pup in for the night. Shaking his head, Luke walked into the bathroom, brushed his teeth, and stood peeing as Nash walked to the door and stared at him.

"What?"

"It's funny how hot you are, and that you don't believe me."

Heat flashed across Luke as he tried to focus on taking care of business. "No new glasses for you."

"I don't wear glasses."

"Then you don't get to have an eye exam."

Nash chuckled as Luke finished, tucked himself back into his briefs, and washed up. As he walked by Nash, he was caught in two strong arms.

"Thanks for being understanding about the dog. I don't know. I just want to take care of him. He seems so helpless."

Luke stiffened for an instant before relaxing into Nash's arms. "It's okay. He is cute. And since you're in charge of him, you get to clean up when he piddles."

Nash chuckled and pulled Luke tight for a kiss, and was rewarded with a bark from across the room. Nash looked toward the dog and chuckled. "Hang on! No one is keeping my attention away from you."

Luke crawled into bed and pulled the sheet over himself. Nash slipped his naked body beside him and looked back with a mischievous grin. "I think you might as well move over to me if you want to cuddle tonight. Because I think I'm going to have to sleep where he can see me or it's going to be a long night."

With a sigh, Luke scooted across the bed and curled against Nash. He heard one soft whimper from Bingo but soon drifted off to sleep.

CHAPTER TEN

NASH STOOD in Luke's yard, the oppressive heat lessening as the daylight faded. The pup ran up to him, threw the ball on the ground, and barked. Nash shook himself from his mood and grinned at his insistent playmate.

"Sorry, bud. I forgot, it's all about you." He grabbed the ball and lobbed it to the far side of the yard. Even the hyperactive puppy couldn't keep him from reflecting on his time on the ranch.

The time had gone by quietly as Luke did the things that needed to be done while Nash nursed Bingo back to health. They ate with Chris a few more times, but she hadn't said any more. The comfort grew between the two of them. Nash came to relish the time they spent together. But the more comfortable they became, the less Nash wanted to ruin everything by telling Luke what he was.

"Hey, dog is walking pretty well."

Nash glanced over to see Luke coming over from the barn. As their gazes met, a broad smile stretched across Luke's face. At the same instant, he felt the familiar bounce of Bingo's nose under his hand, demanding more attention. He studied the puppy's lean frame and realized over the last few days he'd gotten much better.

"Yeah, he's keeping up with me, no problem. I'm amazed that he isn't afraid of the cattle, even that nasty bull you bought."

"Good, that's great. I was afraid he was too badly hurt for your TLC to make any difference. But you've got the touch. No question about that."

Nash studied Luke, not certain how to take the information Luke had shared. "You thought he was going to die?"

Luke laid his hand on Nash's shoulder and squeezed. At the touch a wave of comfort slid through him.

"If I didn't think he had a chance, I would have said something. Letting you bring him home and knowing he was going to die would have been mean." Luke paused and grew thoughtful. "I wasn't sure what was wrong. But I figured you taking care of him would give him a much better chance than otherwise. You had the time to devote to him. More importantly, you wanted him to get better."

"I guess, but he could have died. That would have been horrible."

Luke studied him before he spoke. "It happens, Nash. Everything dies at its own time. No matter how hard you try to save them."

"But the cows don't run up and sniff me or dance around like I'm important."

The sadness that seemed to drape over Luke faded as he began to chuckle. "True, very true. But the important thing is he's frisky and doing well now."

Nash glanced down at the dog, who met his eyes. Bingo's tongue hung from one side of his mouth as he panted. Nash couldn't keep from joining Luke's chuckle. "You crazy dog. Come on, let's go check the insane bull that you should be afraid of."

Luke and Nash made their way to the pen holding the new herd sire. The change of scenery hadn't helped the big animal's disposition. It snorted and charged at the fence. After a few steps, it slid to a stop, snorted again, and pawed dust into the air.

"He's going to hurt you. You bought a crazy bull."

"He's not that bad. You just have to make sure you keep an eye on him any time you're in the pen with him."

"What about after you put him with the girl cows?"

Luke grinned. "Cows are only girls. But if he's still so aggressive, I'll use the pickup when I'm in the pen with him."

"I guess." Nash dropped his gaze to the ground and exhaled.

"What?"

"Tomorrow I have to go back to Atlanta."

This time it was Luke's turn to sigh. "I don't want you to go. I like having you here."

132

"I have to go back. I can't stay gone from my job for long or I won't have it once I get back." He gave Luke a rueful smile. "I don't think you'd want me to live here with you."

Luke stopped and turned back to him. A sense of dread filled Nash. *Oh no, we're not going there. I've seen the "I'm in love with the whore" look too often.*

Nash plunged forward in the conversation so Luke had no chance to speak. "Besides, I have a lease that I can't get out of, and what would I do here?"

Nash chided himself; he'd known this was just a little lark before he'd left Atlanta. In spite of the emotional distance he tried to maintain, he couldn't help but think he needed to warn Luke. He frowned as he considered his options, not liking any of them.

"What?"

He shook off his stupor to find Luke, and the dog, staring at him. "What's wrong?" Luke asked again.

"Nothing. Don't worry about it. Nothing you can do about it." Nash leaned down and scratched the pup behind the ears. "You too, pup. Neither of you need to worry. I've been taking care of myself for a hell of a long time."

Luke shrugged and turned away, but not before Nash caught a glimpse of his expression. He didn't look any happier than Nash felt. But he kept telling himself, they both knew this trip would come to an end. Neither of them had an alternative. Luke turned back and their gazes locked. They stood looking at each other for what felt like hours, but was more likely a few seconds. Luke turned, his face crestfallen as he walked slowly to the house.

Nash sighed softly and ran to catch up. He stepped through the door right behind him. They'd almost made it to the kitchen when Luke turned on him. He looked hurt and angry, neither of which meant this was going to be a pleasant conversation.

"You already know my big secret. But you don't trust me with yours. That really hurts."

"Not now, okay? Please. I'd like my last day to be good."

Luke blew air through his nose and threw his hands in the air. "Okay, okay. I'll leave it alone." He stared at Nash and seemed to deflate. "You're right. I don't want our last day to be an argument. Let's get some lunch."

"What do you have?"

Luke warmed to a change in topic and glanced in the fridge. He looked up and grinned at Nash. "Barbecue. How does that sound?"

Nash lifted an eyebrow and studied Luke. "Where did the barbecue come from? I know you didn't cook it."

"Nope. I wasn't anywhere near it or it would be burned. I gave Chris some money. She brought it out and left it while we were working this afternoon."

"Get that shit on the table, then. I'm starved and so long as it's not your cooking, I'm going to want at least seconds, if not thirds."

Luke reopened the refrigerator, pulled out several containers, and lined them up on the counter. He lifted the lids and the scent of hickory smoke filled the room. He grinned as Nash crowded against him. "Hang on. Just because you got longer arms is no reason to snatch the food."

Nash chuckled as he stuck a rib in his mouth and sucked the meat off. He tossed the stripped bone into the trash before licking his fingers clean. He studied Luke over his hand as he cleaned the last of the sauce. *I hope this truce will last a little longer.* Luke grabbed plates for both of them out of the cabinet, along with a couple of tumblers. A few seconds later their plates were piled high and Luke pulled out a pitcher of what Nash guessed was sangria from the fridge. Nash lifted his eyebrows when Luke looked at him.

"Chris, the sangria was her idea. But I didn't dare complain."

"No, I wouldn't either."

Luke stood and motioned to the porch. "We can go outside and eat if you'd like. We don't get too many eat-outside days in this part of the country."

"Sounds great, and then I don't have to watch the dog as much." As if on cue, Bingo walked past them and out the door. The two men chuckled and followed. They kept up the facade of relaxed

134

conversation, but Nash knew their camaraderie of the previous week was gone.

They finished the meal and sat on the porch until well after dark, progressing from sangria to beer. They both carefully avoided controversial topics as Luke talked about long-term plans for the ranch. The lightning bugs came out for the evening and created patterns that mesmerized Nash.

Nash drank the last of his beer and smiled at Luke. "I can't believe we've been talking for hours. Thanks for sharing so much of your life."

Luke shrugged and smiled. "Sometimes it would be better if I'd keep my mouth shut. But it was fun." Luke began cleaning up the evidence of their evening, and he glanced toward Nash. "Your flight doesn't leave until afternoon, but we still should get some sleep," Luke said. Nash grabbed one of the trash bags and helped with the cleanup. It didn't take much and shortly they were making their way back into the house.

"Leave it on the counter. I'll take care of it later."

Nash nodded and put things where Luke had motioned. Luke flipped off the lights, the living room a familiar obstacle course for him. Nash cursed softly a few times when his shins met some invisible piece of furniture in the darkness.

Nash stopped, getting frustrated. "Could we turn on the—"

Luke flipped on the bedroom light and smiled sadly at Nash. "Sorry. Old habits."

Neither spoke as they stripped out of their clothes, getting ready for bed. By the time Nash finished in the bathroom, Luke was already in bed. He turned off the bathroom light and made his way to his side. *Funny how it has become my side of the bed in such a short time.* He moved close to Luke, intent on cuddling. But Luke tensed at his touch. Nash sighed, the inevitable ending clearly in sight. He turned on the light beside the bed and sat up with the sheet wrapped around him.

"Let's get this over with," Nash said. He knew he had no other choices at this point. This trip was going to become another gray ache that he kept carefully buried.

Luke slowly sat up, scooting until his back was against the headboard. He looked at Nash but kept his silence.

Nash struggled to find some way to make this whole conversation less painful, but nothing he thought of was going to help. He decided to start with the nuts and bolts. He needed Luke to understand he was in danger and needed to take care of himself.

"Okay, let's get this over with," Nash repeated.

Luke nodded. "So what's the big secret?"

"First, you're not going to like this conversation, but I need you to promise me something."

Luke folded his arms over his chest and cocked an eye. "Promise you what?"

"That you'll get tested."

Luke dropped his arms and looked confused. "Tested… for what?"

Nash sighed. "Don't make this harder by playing stupid. You know what I mean."

"For STDs?"

"Yes."

"Okay. I'll get tested." He paused and considered Nash. "Does that mean you have something? Is that the drama?"

"Actually, no. Or at least the last time I got checked I was clean."

"Okay, so nothing I didn't know. We've both been with other guys. It wasn't like I thought you were a virgin."

Nash spit out a bitter laugh. "No, I would be the fucking anti-virgin. But that's not why you need to be tested." He paused again before plunging forward. "When was the last time you were with Bobby?"

Luke scowled, "That's not really any of your business."

"Probably not. But I realized why Bobby looked so familiar. He's been one of my tricks a few times. It wasn't that often, but I knew I'd seen him before."

Luke's expression hardened. "What are you talking about? What do you mean, he's been one of your tricks before?"

"Oh, come on, Luke. You might be country but you're not stupid. You know what I mean. Are you going to make me say it?

Fine. I'm a rent boy. I sell my ass to whoever has the money. Bobby always shelled out quite a bit because, if I remember right, he's got some serious kinks."

The color drained from Luke's face. "You're a...."

"A whore. I make my living having sex. And I've had sex with Bobby. I always play safe, but he could be finding it with some other guys who aren't as careful."

He could see Luke was shaken but trying to make sense of the conversation. "So. You sell… and we've… without." He gulped hard. "Do I owe you something?"

The last shred of humanity wilted and died. "No. You don't owe me anything. This was just a fucking lark. Get out to see how the other people live. It was a hoot. I'm sure I'll remember it for a while. You know, maybe not your name and shit, but the animals were cool."

Luke looked at him as if he'd sprouted horns and a tail, and in his world, that was probably what he thought of Nash. But it didn't matter anymore; this farce was over. He slipped off the bed and found his clothes. Once he'd dressed, he grabbed his bag that had been shifted into the room over the last few days. He flipped on the light and scanned the room for the last of his stuff, then turned back to Luke, who was still watching him with his mouth agape.

"I'll sleep in the guest room tonight. Tomorrow I'll be out of your life forever."

"Wait, wait a minute. I...."

"You slept with a whore, and you're a good Christian boy. I know how this goes down, so let's not drag it out for any longer than we have to. I had my thing, you got a story to tell for the rest of your life. Let's leave it at that."

Nash charged out of the room without giving Luke time to respond. He raced through the door to the guest room, which he hadn't slept in for quite a few nights. Deep down he wanted Luke to come roaring in and tell him it didn't matter, that they could make it work. But Nash knew better.

He searched the room for his stuff but was careful not to take anything of Luke's. Once the initial fury was exhausted, he collapsed on the bed, his body shaking as he fought down tears. He gasped deeply and let it out in a stuttering breath. The first tear rolled down Nash's cheek and he scrubbed it off. As he dropped his hand, a rough tongue licked it. He slid off the bed to wrap his arms around Bingo.

"You damn dog. You're the only one I'm going to miss. I always did like blue-eyed men." He hugged the dog tightly and kissed him on the forehead. "You going to miss me, boy? Because I'm pretty sure your master isn't going to miss me at all."

He looked around to discover it was only a little past midnight. His flight left after noon, but he wasn't staying here and waiting to see what Luke did. He kept telling himself that it was over so far as he was concerned.

Nash buried his face in Bingo's fur and let the tears flow as he waited for the longest night of his life to end.

"WHAT DO you mean he's at the airport? How the fuck could he be at the airport? His goddamn flight doesn't leave until this afternoon." Luke stomped across the narrow confines of Chris's small kitchen, which he'd stormed into earlier on his panicked search for Nash.

Chris crossed her arms and glared. "You finished cussing at me? Because last time I checked this was my house, and I'm not explaining anything if you're going to be an even bigger asshole than you've already managed."

"No! I'm not fucking finished, because you've turned all my plans into shit. Why did you fucking goddamn do that?"

"Okay, enough. You need to leave, or I am. Besides, no one cusses like that. You just sound stupid."

Luke ground his teeth and stared a hole through Chris. But he knew she wasn't making idle threats. If he didn't get things under control, she'd send him home and he'd be worse off than he was now. Time ticked past as Luke tried to calculate how much longer he had to get to the airport before Nash was on his way back to Atlanta. He'd already tried to call and talk to him, but he had no reception again for some damn reason.

He took a deep breath and turned back to Chris. "I'm calm now. Would you please tell me what happened and why you gave Nash a ride to the airport?"

"I took him because he asked. He showed up at my house at some ungodly hour of the morning and set the dog off."

"How'd he get to your house?"

"I'd have thought that was obvious. He walked. He had that nasty duffle bag over his arm, and he looked like he'd been up all night."

"So what'd he tell you happened?"

"Didn't have to tell me. I knew, 'cause he looked like he'd been sucker punched. He finally told you what he does for a living." She stared at Luke. "And you reacted like I figured you would."

Anger rose in Luke. "How would you have reacted if someone you were starting to like told you they sold themselves for a living?"

"It'd depend. But that's not the question. What'd you do?"

"He told me that he was a hooker and Bobby had been a… client. What do you think I did?"

She glared at him until he felt less sure of his indignation. "You can be a real sanctimonious prick sometimes, Luke Meyers."

"He is a *whore*! He had sex for money. My God, what's so hard to understand here?"

"At least he had the good sense to get paid for it. Unlike you putting out for Bobby for years and getting dumped like a load of goose poop. Did you even ask him why he does it? Or did you stare at him like he was fresh cow shit on your boots?"

Luke lifted the ball cap off his head and ran his fingers through his hair. "I gotta go find him. Hopefully I can get him to talk to me. I might have overreacted."

"You think? You *might* have overreacted?" Chris rolled her eyes. "Good luck. I hope you can salvage this one, 'cause I think he loves you."

Luke checked his phone. No reception. He drew back his arm, ready to smash it on the stone wall.

"Two hundred bucks, and they aren't going to buy that you sat on it or the horse stepped on it again. Besides, you're going to need it."

"For what?"

"Because you're about to run out that door to your pickup and drive like hell to the Tulsa airport. And somewhere you'll get a signal and you're going to call Nash and beg for forgiveness."

"I am not going to beg for forgiveness. I just want to talk to him."

"Go with begging for forgiveness. Trust me."

Luke went for the door, ready to acknowledge that Chris was probably right. He'd been a judgmental ass, and he needed to get Nash to give him a second chance. Chris followed, wearing a look he knew all too well.

When they stepped outside, Luke caught a whiff of smoke. He turned to ask Chris if she could smell it too when her house phone began to ring.

Her brows knitted as she stepped over to answer the phone. Luke went outside to see if he could detect anything. There had been a faint wisp of smoke, but he was starting to think he had imagined it when he caught the scent again. He started toward the door when Chris almost knocked him down as she flew out. Grabbing his arm, she dragged him toward the pickup.

"Come on, we gotta go!"

Barely controlled anger and frustration bubbled up inside Luke. "What the hell. Have you lost it?"

"Brush fire on the south end of Tenkiller, and this high wind is sending it right at us. We gotta get going."

Luke's stomach knotted, and it felt like a vise had closed around his heart. But he knew what he had to do, even as a lump formed in his throat. He vaulted into the truck, and they raced toward the volunteer fire department.

NASH SAT with his foot tapping out a fast rhythm on the typical airport floor, becoming more and more eager to be out of this hellhole of a state. He was ready to be back in a place where it rained occasionally and the wind didn't blow constantly. He stared out the window to see waves of heat coming off the runways. He flipped back around, crossed his arms, and slumped into the chair.

"Bad trip?"

Nash glanced over, ready to bite the head off whoever had interrupted his mood, only to discover a woman about the same age his grandmother would be, furiously knitting. She smiled at him and nodded to her flying hands. "Nerves. I hate to fly, so I knit to keep my mind off the fact that tons of metal and people shouldn't be able to fly like a hawk or something. I'll probably have this silly sweater done by the time I make the trip to California and back." The tiny sticks flew back and forth as she studied Nash. "But you don't look anything but unhappy. We're both stuck in this airport, and people say I'm a pretty good listener." She chuckled. "Well, I say I'm a good listener. But then, you'll never see me again, so what do you have to lose?"

Nash's mood was foul enough that he almost turned his frustration on the woman. Fortunately, enough Southern gentleman flowed through his veins that he couldn't bring himself to stoop that low. But he refused to soft pedal it; she'd asked him, after all. "I came here from Atlanta to visit a guy I met online. I knew it couldn't work, but I was stupid enough to come out here anyway."

Her hands stilled as she studied Nash. "Something must have really gone wrong. It sounds like you already knew each other."

Nash shrugged. "I think he was the one who was surprised. I'm tired of being stupid."

"Couldn't talk it out, huh? My husband and I would talk about a problem until we were both so tired that we couldn't even remember the problem."

"Yeah, we talked. I guess. He just kind of stared at me."

Her brows fused together over her eyes. "Young man, you ran off before you talked to your friend. You need to go back and visit with him."

Nash was considering his reply when he heard Stillwell from the television beside where they were sitting. He asked, "Did they say Stillwell? I thought they said something about Stillwell."

She looked up and studied the screen through several cycles. They both heard the newscaster begin a report on an out of control wildfire southwest of Stillwell, near Lake Tenkiller.

Nash knew exactly where the fire was. Racing directly toward Luke's ranch. The angry words they'd exchanged last night no longer mattered. As his fury and hurt melted away, he realized that he still cared for Luke and needed to be there to help as Luke's friend even if it was nothing more. He spun back on the woman. "I need to get to Stillwell. Is there a taxi or something?"

"Oh, hon. This is Oklahoma, not Chicago. Can't you call them?"

Nash looked hopeful, but reality came smashing back into him. "They couldn't come get me now. That fire is going right at two of my friends' ranches."

The woman studied him while panic built for Nash, leaving him pacing ferociously. He had to get back somehow. "I'll have to hitch my way back."

"Heavens, my sister is going to kill me. But this is an emergency." The woman started gathering up her knitting and carefully, but quickly, putting it away. In a few seconds, she stood and looked at Nash. "Well? You ready?"

Is she really offering me what it sounds like? "Ready? What?"

"To go back to Stillwell to help your friend. I'd say you need to help save his ranch and have a long talk. But you can't walk there. This'll give me a chance to put off getting in that nasty plane."

The almost extinguished flicker of hope burned brighter as Nash followed the woman to her car.

Chapter Eleven

"Well, I'll be damned," said Chris as she studied the latest load of people coming to help fight the fire.

Luke followed her gaze as he leaned against the grassfire truck, trying to wash several hours of soot and smoke from his throat. He flipped up the bottle of water and almost spewed it out on the ground when he saw Nash walk toward them.

The man he hadn't expected to see ever again stood before them.

Nash stopped a few feet in front of him and crossed his arms. "This doesn't mean we don't still have a lot to talk about. But I saw the fire on the airport TV, and I came to help."

Luke glanced at Chris to find her staring at him. Knowing he wasn't going to get any latitude from that corner, he turned back to Nash and nodded agreement. "Yes, after. I… after."

Nash looked around the staging area before glancing back at Luke. "I got a ride from the airport and jumped in a pickup that was heading out. Where are we? Where's the fire?"

"We're about twenty miles south of the house. Some stupid city kid decided all the no fires signs didn't mean him when he was camping on the lake." A gust of wind hammered them, forcing Luke to grab his hat before the wind blew it away. "The weather's not helping either. The whole damn place is a tinderbox, and the fire is headed right at us."

Nash glanced at the gathering of volunteer firefighters before shifting his gaze back to Luke. "What do you want me to do? I don't have the gear most of you have."

"We could use some help on the pumper truck. Some of those folks have been at it since early morning."

Nash studied the squat truck with the ledge in the front and nodded. "Okay, I can do that."

NASH TROTTED to the truck and climbed on the front. The driver tossed him a harness, which he gladly buckled himself into. Using it, he fastened himself to the truck's platform. Nash gave it a few tugs to make sure it was secure before he turned to see who had joined him to man the hoses.

"Hey, looks like it could be a busy day."

It took all of Nash's control not to let his mouth drop open, because the person standing beside him was none other than Bobby Doyle. He stared into the man's face, trying to figure out what to say, then realized Bobby had already spoken to him.

"Yeah, it's going to be busy. Hopefully we can get this thing stopped."

"That'd be good. Although if it all burned, it wouldn't be a huge loss. Mostly scrub oak and blackjacks for miles in any direction."

Nash clenched his jaw. "There are people who live out here too."

"Oh, we'll get it stopped long before it gets close to anyone's house." Bobby buckled himself onto the rail before turning back to Nash. "You know, you look familiar. I can't quite place you, though."

"Maybe if your head was buried in a pillow it would come to you," Nash muttered.

Bobby spun around. "What'd you say?"

The driver tossed them a couple of packs, stopping the conversation between Nash and Bobby. "Put 'em on. There's a foil blanket that might help if you get trapped by the fire. There's also a brush knife. You shouldn't need any of it, not with being on the truck, but we like to play it safe."

Nash nodded as he looped his arms through the straps and grabbed the rail as they took off. He glanced back to see Luke and Chris sitting in the back of another pickup going the opposite direction. They quickly threaded their way onto a nearly impassible road. The truck shifted into four-wheel drive and slowed to a crawl

144

over the obstacles. As they covered the body-pounding miles, the smoke thickened around them.

They climbed into an open area that ran at least to the next ridge. Now there was no question about the location of the fire; he could see the tongues of orange a few hundred yards inside the tree line.

"This is it! We need to keep it out of the opening or it will jump the next road. Grab the hoses and drench everything. This shouldn't be too bad."

Nash pulled the hose from its reel and, after a moment of fumbling, turned it on. Bobby's came on a minute or so later. The truck eased forward as they soaked the dry tinder along the tree line. They splashed through a small creek at the base of the next hill and made their way to the top of the ridge. By the time they turned and found their way back to the starting point, Nash could hear the crackle of the fire.

"Shit. The wind's picking up. Keep an eye out for anything blowing behind us." They sprayed water in a broad swath, catching those few embers that blew from the trees to land in the dry grass. Nash used his sleeve to wipe the sweat off his forehead, exposing the tattoo covering his arm. Bobby glanced at it and studied Nash for a moment before his face bleached white.

Nash gave him a wolfish grin, wishing for once in his life he did have fangs he could bare. He leaned closer to Bobby. "Remember me now?"

At that instant, they topped the hill to find themselves in a fire devil. The howling winds and column of fire slammed into them, and the driver cranked the wheel in an attempt to get away. The crew was barely able to hold on as the truck careened downhill. A final swerve threw them into a tangle of straps and bodies on the fire bridge of the truck. One of the straps ended up across Nash's throat, cutting off his air. His vision began to dim, and he dug for the knife. He yanked it from the pack, wedged the blade under the strap, and sawed. The right one parted, and Nash coughed as he gasped for air. The truck lurched again, and he was tossed from the platform.

He landed with enough impact to knock out what little air he'd retained. An instant later he realized Bobby had been thrown too, and lay beside him, stunned. The heat bore down on Nash from all sides, and when he looked to the south, there was nothing but a wall of orange roaring toward them.

He spotted a stream at the bottom of the hill and knew that was their only hope. He looked at Bobby and contemplated leaving him behind. *He's a world-class asshole. Why should I save him?* Then he let out a held breath, knowing he couldn't do that to anyone.

He grabbed Bobby by the shirt and dragged him down the hill and toward the stream as fast as possible. By the time he got Bobby into the water, his clothing was beginning to smolder. He pulled Bobby into the stream, then dropped beside him, soaking them both. The heat against his face was almost unbearable. He splashed water over his head and the burning stopped for a second. He tried to do the same with Bobby's softly groaning figure, but he realized they were close to being overcome. Then he remembered the packs and ripped through them as he pulled Bobby beside him, covering them with the foil blankets until Bobby struggled and screamed out, "God help us! We're going to die! We're going to die!"

"Shut your fucking trap and lay still. Don't make me regret that I dragged you down here." Terror-filled eyes locked on him. "I swear, you fight me again and I'll knock you in the head with a rock," Nash said.

Bobby whimpered and tried to press himself against Nash. "My legs are burning. It's getting hot. I can barely breathe."

"Splash water on yourself and keep your face just above the water so you can get the coolest air. Try to keep the blankets wrapped over us."

A huge cedar tree exploded into flames a few yards away, shooting burning fragments in all directions. Bobby was frightened beyond his ability to speak. The foil began to give under the heat, but Nash refused to give up. He squirmed against the streambed, trying to get a little more of his body covered, and dunked his head to keep it from burning. The pain approached unbearable as he fought to keep them both wet. The foil parted and Nash closed his eyes, waiting for the fire to overcome them.

Another evergreen flared above them, but the heat didn't seem to intensify. He kept splashing, trying to keep skin and clothing wet for them both, but the fire seemed to have reached its peak. Nash knew how his luck usually went and figured it was about to run out— for the last time.

But instead, the wind stilled and after a few seconds, Nash recognized the heat was less intense. He didn't dare look up, and he knew his precious hair was singed beyond belief, but he was still alive. As everything started to calm down, Nash relaxed. About the same time, Bobby wriggled from under him. Nash realized the burning now was from his already overexposed skin and not from the fire that had passed over them.

He sat up, letting the slow flowing stream travel over him as he looked around them. It was a scene straight out of one of those disaster movies that ended with everything black and charred. Live coals were piled among the trees.

"I didn't think we were going to make it. Ah, thanks. You know."

Nash scowled and shook his head. "Don't get all sappy about it. I'm not sure what happened."

"Yeah, okay. I guess I owe you."

"You don't owe me anything. But if you'd quit tormenting Luke, I'd consider it a personal favor."

A smirk appeared on Bobby's face.

"This would not be the time to get a smartass mouth. Not unless you want your wife to know you pay extra for a pounding that gives you a hands-free come," Nash said.

A voice came from above them. "Hey! You guys okay?"

LUKE WALKED through the dark house and into the bathroom to check on Nash. He cringed at the sight. Nash looked like he had the worst case of sunburn Luke had ever seen. He tried to ease the linen cabinet open without disturbing him.

"You might as well come sit down so we can talk about shit. 'Cause I don't plan on getting out of the cold bath until I'm wrinkled as a fucking prune."

Luke caught Nash's gaze and saw him glance toward the toilet. He stepped over, lowered the lid, and sat down. "This isn't exactly where I thought this talk would happen."

A whine came from the door and two more eyes stared at Luke. "Come on, Bingo. You might as well be involved too. You weren't happy your boss was gone this morning." Bingo looked first at Nash and then Luke before slipping next to the toilet and dropping his head onto his paws.

Once the dog was settled, Luke turned back to Nash with a sigh. "I'm sorry about last night. I didn't handle it like I should. I was stupid."

"You were being stupid because I'm a sex worker. I could have told you I worked for the mob and you would have reacted better."

"No! Well. I don't think so."

"See. It's the whole sex thing. And what changed your mind?"

"Chris...."

"And what'd she say?"

Luke looked over and studied the water Nash was floating in. "You need some cooler water? The doc said this would help the burn."

"That bad, huh?"

Luke dropped his hands to his knees and his body sagged. "You aren't going to let this go, are you?"

"Nope."

"Fine. She said at least you got paid for it. That I was Bobby's whore for years and never got a dime."

"He pays extra for some things." Nash covered his mouth with his hand and held it for a moment before letting it slip off. "Sorry. I guess I'm still more pissed off than I realized."

"I had it coming." Luke sat quietly for some time, staring into his hands.

Nash pushed his fingers through the water and watched as the ripples went down the tub. "What else?"

Luke twisted his head and met Nash's gaze. "He never wanted to do anything beyond oral and hand jobs with me."

Nash considered him and sank into the cool water. As he lifted his head, he ran his hands over his sheared scalp. "It feels weird to not have my hair. Dammit, it looked hot too."

Before he thought, Luke reached over and ran his hand over Nash's closely sheared head. The short pieces of hair were certainly a different sensation from the ponytail Nash wore before. Chris had done the honors of cutting Nash's hair, and she did Luke's too. The two styles looked a lot alike.

Luke realized his touch might not be welcome. But as he pulled back, another thought occurred to him. "Did any of your piercings burn you? I know some of the dark parts of your tattoos are blistered."

Nash grinned mischievously and floated to the surface, his cock shriveled against him. "You want to check for burns?"

Luke's cheeks heated up but before he could reply, Nash's face turned sour and he sank his midsection to the bottom of the tub. "Sorry, I lost it for a minute. I guess I'm like one of the unclean in your book now."

Sadness with a touch of loneliness filled Luke. "You have to give me a little time to take it in. I thought you sold magazines door to door or something. You always avoided telling me what you did. But we do need to talk, and if you get out of the tub, you're going to be miserable."

"No, I make a hell of a lot more than those guys. But I guess it's more dangerous. The black eyes and bruises I had when I got here was from a guy who beat on me. The cops don't care about hookers getting beat up either. I was hospitalized. It was a bad scene." He turned to look at Luke. "Ask your questions. It isn't like it could get much worse at this point."

Luke hesitated, not sure he wanted to go down this path. But he also knew he had strong feelings for Nash before all this happened. He braced himself and asked what had been bothering him the most.

"Why do you do it? You're a smart guy, and easy to talk to. Why sell yourself?"

"I never finished high school, and I was only fifteen when I ended up in Atlanta. One of the soldiers at the local base had been pounding me since I was fourteen. I'd asked him to get me beer, but he didn't want money in exchange. Then I got caught and thrown out. My wonderful father said he'd shoot me if he saw me again. So I ran, to Atlanta. I'd used up every dime I had by the time I got there. I was too young to get a real job. A guy at the shelter told me about a way to make money." Nash shrugged again. "Some like 'em young. Pay extra. But I can't pass for a kid anymore."

"Why? I mean, I get that you don't look fifteen. Don't you just get guys that like older guys?" Luke felt the flush cover him at the direction the conversation was taking. "I mean. Fifteen-year-olds don't do anything for me, but you…."

Nash turned in the tub and put his chin on the porcelain. "You're a sweet guy. But guys that hire me now, well, tattoos and piercings are generally a turn-on for a rougher crowd."

Luke tried to imagine how Nash's life had been. "This wasn't the first time you've been hurt, was it?"

Nash rolled on his back and sank into the water. Luke thought he wasn't going to answer when Nash began to speak. "No, it wasn't the first. Some of the tattoos are to cover scars. I think they're beautiful works of art, and I have them with me all the time. But that's not how most people see them."

Luke slipped off the toilet seat and knelt beside the tub. "I don't know what will happen. I'm not sure what we are to each other. But I do know you're a guy I want to get to know better. Please stick around a few more days. You don't want to be on a plane with most of your body burned and tender anyway, do you?"

Nash turned so they faced each other. "I wasn't looking forward to the flight to Atlanta when I can barely stand to have clothes touch me." He took a deep breath and continued. "But I'm sleeping in the guest room. You need some space to decide what you want. I'll be honest, I don't think it will work out. I don't see how I could ever fit in here."

Luke's chest tightened at the words, and he wished he could shout his disagreement. But he knew they were different and from wildly divergent backgrounds. But he'd hoped. He had hoped so hard. "Okay, if that's what you want. I'd like it if you'd stay around for another few days."

Nash's mouth drew into a thin line. Then he glanced to Luke. "What about the fire? How is everything? When they hauled me off, it was still spreading."

"The wind dropped at sunset, and they think we might have it under control. It got pretty close. I'd say a half mile as the crow flies. We got lucky. A couple of families south of us lost their houses."

"And Bobby?" It pained Nash to ask, but his curiosity won out.

Luke's voice filled with loathing. "He's much better off than you. Apparently he hid under you. Worthless shit."

What was left of Nash's eyebrows shot up. "The crown prince of Stillwell has crashed and burned?"

A bitter taste filled Luke's mouth. "He wouldn't tell us what happened at first. He kept saying he'd saved you and that you might have brain damage. But the fire marshal cornered him and finally made him admit you'd rescued him. He's a useless asshole."

"He likes them young. Very young."

"Bobby likes boys?"

"I don't know. But he hired me more often when I was a kid. He even paid for my first tattoo." He showed Luke a red koi on his arm. "But he always was creepy, and I don't think he's been around for a year or so. I think I got too old for him."

Luke sat quietly, trying to figure out where the new piece of information went with everything else from the years he'd been Bobby's hookup. He lifted his head slowly and ran his tongue over his lips as he worked up enough courage for a last question.

"Do you mind if I ask a personal question?"

Nash looked at him with a sad smile. "I think we're long past worrying about a question being too personal. Ask whatever you want."

"Did you like it?"

Nash stilled himself in the tub and sat without speaking until Luke decided he wasn't going to answer. Then Nash whispered, "Sometimes. Sometimes it felt like they cared and it was good. No one cares about their hooker, but they made it feel like they did. Then there were times when it was so bad I couldn't get hard." He locked eyes with Luke. "Recently, it's been a lot more of the bad ones."

CHAPTER TWELVE

NASH BUTTONED the cuffs of a long-sleeved shirt he'd borrowed from Luke as he made his way from the house to the barn. Things were still tense between the two of them, but they had talked the whole thing to death at this point. Luke looked up as he led his horse and Jack out of the stables. They heard the puppy whining and barking to be released from the stall Luke had put him in so he wouldn't follow Nash. Bingo had managed to get his feet burned, and Luke didn't want the injury to become worse.

"You don't have to go, you know."

Nash nodded as he took the reins to the mule and walked beside Luke. "I know, but this shouldn't be a big deal. Just riding around and checking for hot spots." He patted the saddlebags Luke had packed for them. "And if I find something, I give the firefighter guys a call."

"Actually, your phone probably won't work. Reception's always spotty here, and the fire took out one of the cell towers. But anything that's left you should be able to take care of."

A case of nerves flowed through Nash, but he refused to let Luke see it. "Sounds good. You said we should be finished by lunch?"

"I'd think so. It shouldn't take more than a couple of hours. Just throwing a little dirt on any hot spots."

"Okay, sounds pretty easy." Nash watched as Luke took a couple of tries before he made it into the saddle of his lunging horse. Once he was settled into place, Nash turned to the mule.

Nash stared intently at the animal. "Are you planning something like that? Because if you are, I'd just as soon fall from here." Jack looked away and snorted, his hide twitching away a fly but otherwise as still as a rock. Nash put one foot in the stirrup and paused. When there was no movement, he slowly put weight on it and threw his leg over the saddle. He fished for the other stirrup, and Jack stood like granite until Nash was seated, then strolled over to Luke.

"I wish I knew what you and that dang mule have. He's never that calm with anyone else."

"I don't know. He's always seemed pretty reasonable."

Luke tilted his hat back and scratched his head before continuing. "We're ready, I guess. Jack'll keep you out of trouble. You can trust him."

"You said follow the fence over there." Nash pointed to a section of fence that had to be at least forty years old.

"Yup, ride along it and you'll go in a big loop that comes back to the house. I don't think much of the fire even got this far, if any. But I thought it would be good to check."

"Okay, sounds pretty easy. I'll see you at lunch."

A FEW hours passed as Nash and the mule slowly made their way along the fence. They'd gone through a couple of old gates, and he was beginning to wonder if they were lost. He didn't think it had taken this long for them to make their way around the pasture when he and Luke had been together.

He reached down and patted the mule's neck. "Dude, I appreciate the ride and all. But I gotta take a leak." As if he understood, the mule slowed to a stop, swung his head, and stared at Nash.

"Well okay. That was easy enough."

He swung his leg over the saddle and lowered himself. But when his foot touched the ground, his legs and butt screamed as cramped muscles unwound from several hours of riding. He grabbed the cantle and buried his face against Jack's flank. The pain subsided and he lurched away from the mule and stumbled a few feet. He waited for the pain to subside again and took another step.

"Damn, Jack. Why didn't you tell me I should have gotten off and walked more?"

The mule stared at him and snorted before starting to graze. Nash watched him and unzipped his pants. "I might as well take care

of draining the wiener, hadn't I, boy. I don't need to walk to do that."
He fished his dick out of the open fly, pointed it downwind, and took
care of long overdue business. The wind flipped through with a fitful
twist and Nash detected a hint of smoke in the air. He quickly tucked
himself back in his jeans and took a few steps in the direction the
scent came from.

He stood quietly before turning toward his ride. "You smell
that? I think there might actually be fire. Let's go check it out."

He moved to get back into the saddle, but stopped and smiled at
the mule. "If you don't mind, I think I'll walk for a little while."

Nash followed the growing odor of smoke as they searched. By
the time he could smell it strongly, they'd reached one of the oldest
fences Nash had ever seen. The posts were obviously cut from the
surrounding trees and had weathered to a light gray with a filigree of
gray-green lichens from top to bottom. But when Nash pushed against
it, he discovered it was still a solid obstacle.

He studied the problem, trying to find a way to get them both
over the fence. Then he remembered Luke's comment about Jack
being trained to be a jumping mule. "So you've been trained to jump
fences, big feller. Let's see if Luke set us up."

He dropped the mule's reins, walked back, and went through his
saddlebags. The first side was nothing but first aid medicines, with a
healthy supply of burn ointment. "Well I guess he was worried about
my delicate skin."

He ducked in front of the mule and opened the other pouch.
"That's better. Just what we needed." Nash pulled out a blanket and
unfolded it. Jack watched him as he stepped between two of the posts
and laid the blanket over the wire. He stepped back to survey the
visible barrier and gathered the reins again. He looked at the mule for
a minute, then Jack took a few steps and stopped in front of the fence
before turning his head toward Nash.

"Oh, I guess I need to be on the other side, huh."

He straddled the fence, getting caught for a few seconds on the
barbs, but got free with only a small rip in the crotch of his pants.

He ran his hand over his crotch and grinned at Jack. "Family jewels intact, check. Now, how do we get you over the fence?"

The mule flicked his ears and moved from side to side. Nash retreated to the end of the reins when the mule rose on his back legs and shoved himself forward. Nash's jaw dropped as Jack cleared the fence with no apparent effort. He took a couple of steps forward and flipped both ears toward Nash.

"Oh, shut the fuck up. You aren't that good. And I'm ready to ride again, so there."

Nash stepped to the mule's left and managed to get into the saddle and only wanted to scream a little from the pain. They traveled at an easy pace as Nash scrutinized the surroundings. When the trees and brush became thicker, Jack slowed his pace accordingly. The smell of smoke was slowly growing, but something grated on Nash's nerves. He stopped the nervous chatter with the mule as they moved farther from the ranch house.

Jack forced their way through a particularly dense patch of cedars while Nash deflected the branches. They stepped into a relatively open area and Nash checked their surroundings. The trees had been trimmed up the trunks, creating the illusion of openness. A second later, he realized there was some kind of dark netting hung from the trees surrounding him. He slowly dismounted and led the mule closer. He pushed back the netting with one hand to find a cluster of pot plants under it.

"Holy shit!" said Nash.

"Don't move."

The voice came from behind him, no way to do anything. *I hate this more than anything I can think of. I hate it when someone has me like this.*

"Look, I was making sure there are no hot spots from yesterday's fire. I smelled some smoke and came to check. I swear I wasn't getting into anybody else's business. Just let me go and I won't mention this to anyone."

Nash lifted his hands and slowly turned toward the source of the voice. "Hey, really, I don't care what you're doing. You don't want to hurt anyone. Come on, let me go." Nash finally turned to find the guy standing behind him. It was the crazy man who'd threatened them on the road beside Luke's house. "Look, I swear. It'll be our secret." Nash fought to keep his emotions under control as the agitated man stood with a pistol trained on him.

The silence stretched on too long, and Nash decided to try again. "Hey man, let's be cool about this. So you make a little extra cash selling weed. Who cares? A little pot never hurt anyone."

"Shut up! Shut up so I can think."

The guy yanked the gun around, and from Nash's viewpoint it was a cannon. His captor wildly scanned the area around them, obviously afraid someone was with Nash. He became more and more frantic and the wild swinging of his gun was not helping Nash stay calm.

"Hey, man, it's just me. No one else is here."

The lunatic swung to him, the gun unstable, and screamed, "I said shut up!" He aimed the gun at Nash's leg and fired.

The next thing Nash knew, he was flat on his back, screaming in pain. The waves of agony were overwhelming as he grabbed the leg and tried to stem the blood. He stared at the man. "You shot me! You fucking shot me!"

He lifted the gun and pointed it at Nash's head.

LUKE CHECKED his watch again. *Almost two o'clock. Where in the world is Nash?* He got up from his kitchen table and walked to the window to stare out again.

"Where is he? It shouldn't take this long."

Chris sipped her coffee before she answered. "I have no idea. Same answer I've given you the last ten times you asked."

He turned away from the window and met Chris's gaze. "I'm not waiting any longer. I need to go find him."

Chris took another sip as she stared over the rim of her cup. "So you're being a good Christian and saving the sinful whore?"

Luke's eyes narrowed. "You can be a real bitch when you want to be, can't you?"

"Answer the question."

Luke tightened his jaw, his anger at the whole situation flaring until he was ready to bite nails. "We're talking. I don't know what'll happen. You know my track record."

"Bullshit."

"Why are you doing this? Do you want me pissed off? We're just wasting time."

Chris stared at him and shrugged.

Luke stomped out the back door, slamming the screen door behind him. He was halfway to the stables when he heard the door close again, but he was too angry with Chris to have any kind of discussion. He led his horse out of the stall, into the tack room, and grabbed a pad and saddle.

Chris took her horse out and started saddling it, but Luke was mounted and headed for the gate before she emerged from the stables. The dog was barking so furiously that Chris opened the stall door and let him out. He sprinted after Luke like a gray streak.

Before Luke made his way through the first gate, she'd put her horse into a trot and caught up. Luke ignored her under the pretext of examining the ground for some kind of trail. The dog running ahead and then back wasn't helping him calm down.

"You do know that I'm smart enough to understand you aren't going to find shit in these hoofprints by the house where everything comes up for water."

"Never know."

Chris dropped back a yard or two and trailed behind Luke. He kept his horse at a fast walk as they traveled along one of the boundary fences. They came to the final corner of Luke's property and he studied the gate before slipping off his horse to look closer.

"What?"

"I think he went through the gate. Why would he do that?"

Chris nudged her mount closer and studied the area while Luke walked a few yards away.

158

"He went this way. There are fresh tracks." Luke backtracked to the corner and studied each bit of it. He went over it carefully, inch by inch, until he found what he was looking for.

"The post is so rotten the staples that kept it from being opened fell out. Grandpa put the gates in so it would be easier to get stray livestock back inside."

"So he thought it was one of your gates and went through it?"

"That's what it looks like. Dammit."

"Sure are anxious to find a slut."

"Enough. All right?"

Chris shrugged and rode through the gate while Luke held it open. They traveled silently as worry built in Luke. He knew Nash was lost, whether Nash knew it or not. He also knew they were too close to the Koslov place, and Ian Koslov was crazy.

Time stretched as they spent hours looking for Nash, trailing along ancient fences, backtracking up washes and ravines until Luke was becoming desperate. They threaded their way through a particularly dense patch of trees, and Luke thought he heard something.

"Hang on. Stop."

They both brought their mounts to a halt and sat quietly listening.

"Nothing. I guess I was wanting it too badly."

They pushed to an opening in the dense cover and Luke spotted something that filled him with both joy and horror. Jack ran to them in that shuffling gait mules sometimes use—without Nash. As the mule got close, Bingo loped over to him, sniffed the animal, and started running sweeps in the dense grass and last year's leaves.

"Dammit! Where's he at?" Luke asked.

"Where are we?"

Luke glanced at Chris. "Somewhere in the back part of the Koslov place."

Their gazes met and Luke fished out his phone without hesitation and handed it to Chris. "Usually you can get a signal at that ridge we crossed a mile or so ago. Call the sheriff directly, his number's on my phone. Tell him we have a problem and where we are. Get them here as quick as possible. This whole thing is making my skin crawl."

"Got it." She stuck the phone in a zippered pocket, spun her horse, and disappeared into the brush. Without hesitation he turned back, swung off his horse, and dropped the reins.

"I hope you don't forget what ground tied is. But there's no way you could jump this fence without being able to take a run at it." He turned from the horse, slipped through the fence without a problem, and stood looking at the mule.

"Please let's have a good day. If something's happened to Nash, it won't be good. You can get me there a lot faster than I can walk." He looked over to the dog, who was still searching the area. "Maybe you can help too." The mule rolled its eyes as Luke walked closer, but never moved as he swung into the saddle. He waited a few seconds to see what was going to happen, but Jack stood steady.

Luke turned to the dog, who was becoming more desperate with each passing moment. "Okay, Bingo. You want to pretend you're a dang bloodhound or something? Find Nash. Come on, boy. Find your master."

Bingo tucked his cocked ears behind his head, then flicked them forward as Luke talked to him. Then he tilted his head at Luke, spun, and took off at full speed away from the fence.

"Holy shit. That dog can run."

He reappeared a few yards ahead of them and shot Luke a flurry of barks before plunging back into the brush. The mule followed at a ground-eating lope while Luke tried to watch for Nash. The trees had again become almost impassible when the dog ran to his side, but this time he moved silently. *This doesn't feel right. I think I'll take it easy from here.*

Luke slipped out of the saddle and eased into the tangle of scrub oak, green briar, and cedar. As he pulled the foliage apart, he gasped. Luke pulled back, working to move as quietly as possible. He knew what netting like that was used for, and he'd never seen a pot farm as big as what was carefully tucked in the clearing a few yards from him.

He had no doubt what had happened to Nash. His gut cramped as he let himself consider the possibilities.

NASH SAT as still as possible to keep the pain to tolerable levels. The look on the guy's face when he'd pointed the gun at Nash's head still made him want to puke. He kept walking past and mumbling. If Nash hadn't been in so much pain and worried about the amount of blood he'd lost, it would have caused him serious worry. As it was, the blood from the hole in his leg had drenched his jeans and his head was starting to swim. It wasn't going to matter much longer whether he shot him again or not.

"Hey, what're you doing? I told you to not move."

"Man, I couldn't move if I wanted to. I can barely sit up."

Nash sensed the gun being pointed at him again, but he refused to look up. He pressed as hard as he could stand against the wound, but the blood still seeped between his fingers. The fact that it was a hot, sunny afternoon but he felt cold did nothing to comfort him.

He drifted and watched the crazy pot dealer running back and forth. He seemed to be gathering things up and throwing them into a pickup that had seen far more years than Nash. The man's movements were jerky and hesitant, which did nothing to calm Nash's already failing system. The fog Nash's mind swam in cleared, and he considered the area around him, wondering if there was a way out. But he was sure the mule had run off with the gunshot, and he couldn't conceive of a way to escape on foot.

He heard the madman talking to himself on the other side of the clearing. "Where's the bag of compost? Gotta have the stuff for next place. Seeds. Seeds too. Can't come back. Have to get all the important stuff." He walked off as he continued to chatter to himself.

Nash glanced around, determined to use the moment of clarity. The only cover he could find was a dozen yards behind him. What normally wouldn't have taken more than a second or two to cross looked like miles. But if he was going to die, it wasn't going to be from bleeding to death with his face in the dirt. He braced himself with his good leg and pushed backward an inch or two.

Nash gritted his teeth against the pain, his breath hissing out. Still determined, he pushed again, this time covering more ground. His focus became each shove of his foot and creeping closer to cover. As he moved, he made every attempt to hide the trail he was leaving, but his main focus was on escape. Rational thought left him as he concentrated only on the next move. He shoved again, and low-hanging branches scraped along his neck, poking into the back of his head.

He looked around and realized he'd reached the small thicket he'd spotted. He could hear the voice coming back around the netting and Nash shoved himself inside. His injured leg caught once and the pain that shot through him left him shaking and nauseous on the litter inside the small copse of trees. He curled in a ball, hoping he was hidden enough.

The footsteps stopped and there was a frantic scuffle of feet as the guy ran back and forth. "You son of a bitch! I'm going to kill you this time. You cocksucking son of a bitch."

Nash cringed at gunfire that sent a bullet whining over his head. Several shots followed, but were more distant. There was a brief period of quiet before Nash heard a peculiar metallic sound that he didn't recognize. He shifted slowly, protecting his leg while he eased the leaves open with his hand. The sight in front of him didn't provide any comfort. Koslov had a machete in one hand and his pistol in the other, and he attacked the small clumps of brush with a terrifying ferocity.

"You shit ass. I'm going to chop you into pieces. You're not going to turn me over to the damn cops. I'm going to be so fucking rich that I have a new woman every night. You're not going to get away."

Nash dodged back, moving to the deepest part of the thicket, and hoped he would somehow miss him. Several minutes passed and the sounds moved away. Nash dropped his head against the ground and prayed for the first time in a long time. He wanted to survive this lunatic and, almost as much, he wanted to get a second chance with Luke.

Then the sound he'd been dreading came. The whine of steel against wood as Koslov used the machete to cut away the branches around him. Nash pulled his legs as tight as possible and waited for the inevitable. The blade landed too close, clipped his side, and brought a new wave of pain. He bit his lip to keep from screaming, but it did little good. The next solid cut released the main branch covering him and it fell to the side.

The man's visage was a study in insanity as he tossed the machete aside. Nash watched stoically while Koslov lifted the pistol and gripped it with both hands. Nash found himself looking down a gun barrel that looked like it was the size of a fifty-five-gallon drum.

"You're a dead man."

CHAPTER THIRTEEN

BINGO HOVERED at Luke's side. The dog had refused to stay with the mule. He could hear Koslov carrying on a continual monologue that highlighted his agitation. Luke had never seen him without a gun, so he knew he couldn't count on dealing with an unarmed man as he moved around the perimeter of the grounds.

He paused to get his bearings and couldn't help but be amazed at the huge number of pot plants. Luke had helped bust a few growers as one of the volunteer deputies. But this was a whole new situation and anything worth as much as the pot around him… well, Luke hoped he was wrong about Nash stumbling into this mess.

He waited, the dog silent beside him, as he searched the area for Nash. Koslov started walking back just as Luke caught a bit of movement at a small thicket of trees. It was Nash's shoe. He was certain of it. Why had he crawled into the brush, though?

An instant later, the lunatic returned, screaming hysterically. The threats removed any doubt that he didn't know Nash was there. And it was obvious when he found Nash, the results were going to be fatal.

When Koslov grabbed a machete and began hacking at any bit of cover Nash might be using to hide, Luke knew it wouldn't be long. His tension eased up when Koslov moved away from Nash's hiding place. Luke crept closer, hoping he could grab Nash and get him out. He'd made it to a few yards away when Koslov rushed the clump hiding Nash and hacked at the thicket of branches.

Luke moved closer as quickly as he could, unsure how he was going to take down the knife-wielding maniac. With another swing of the blade, the situation went from bad to horrible. Koslov had a .38 pointed at Nash, screaming about killing him.

Time was up. He wasn't going to lose Nash to an armed lunatic. Luke lurched from his hiding place, found his goal, and sprinted toward the madman. The years of wrestling practice and thousands of bales of hay thrown into dozens of barns gave him the strength and agility to cover the distance in a heartbeat. He slammed into Koslov's side and they both became airborne for several feet before crashing to the ground. Luke grabbed for the gun as they fought.

They struggled with the gun as it went off again, the bullet embedding itself into a tree that was far too close to Nash. Koslov managed to twist under Luke, grab him by the throat, and squeeze with the strength of a madman. Luke fought to break the hold while still struggling over the gun. A growling streak of gray and white shot over him, and in the next instant Koslov screamed.

"Help! Get the fucking dog off me."

Luke heard a deep growl as the grip on his throat disappeared, and he realized Bingo had his teeth clamped on Koslov's wrist. The dog released his hold and snarled as he lunged at Koslov's throat and face.

Luke took advantage of the distraction and had little trouble knocking the gun to the ground. He grabbed Koslov's arm and cranked it behind his back, wedging it between his shoulder blades as Koslov howled at Bingo's attack. He glanced around and spotted a bundle of zip ties Koslov had used to string the netting through the trees. He grabbed the largest one and tightened it around one wrist. He repeated the motion with the other arm and soon had him immobilized. He twirled Koslov around and shoved him to the ground.

"Please do something stupid. Give me a good reason to shoot you with your own gun."

With that Luke sprinted back to find Nash had not moved. His heart clenched at the sight. One leg of Nash's jeans was soaked with blood, and the cut in his side bled freely. Luke ripped his belt off and tied it as tight as he could above the bullet wound. He knelt, looking helplessly when Nash's eyes fluttered open. Nash wore a lopsided grin.

"I must be in heaven 'cause there's an angel standing over me."

Luke couldn't help but laugh as he eased Nash's head into his lap. "You are so delusional."

"Nah, just a big ole slut."

"Shut up. I happen to love that slut."

He looked up as a white four-wheel drive SUV slid to a stop not far from them. Several more arrived in short order, and soon a bewildering assortment of uniformed men with guns surrounded them. He smiled down at Nash. "The cavalry's arrived. Hang on a little more."

"If I hang on, we can talk about this loving me thing?"

The sirens filled the air as the ambulance pulled as close as they could. When Luke looked back, Nash was unconscious.

"Yes. Oh yes, we're going to talk about the loving you thing."

NASH FOLDED his arms over his chest and stared out the window with Bingo at the spot that was his assigned position since he'd been released from the hospital. He'd had the same look of frustration for the last few days. Luke understood the confinement was wearing on Nash more than it would most people. But at some point, they needed to have the conversation Nash seemed determined to avoid.

"I'm tired of all this crap. I feel fine. My leg feels fine. Cut the damn stitches and yank them out. It can't be that bad. There isn't much to it."

Luke made another glass of sweet tea. He'd learned to make it from Nash's instructions during his week of recovery. It had been a lot more involved than Luke would have ever guessed. He had a feeling it was that difficult in large part because Nash was being an ass. But he was alive and because of that, Luke didn't care how cranky he was. He walked over, handed Nash the tea, and knelt beside the couch. He pushed the leg of the loose shorts they'd found for Nash to wear up until he could see the row of small stitches.

He studied the wound carefully before sighing. "Okay, fine. We'll take out the stitches and put some more antibiotic stuff on it. But you still have to use the crutches if we're going outside."

Luke located a pair of small scissors, tweezers, and the ointment. A little later he'd removed the stitches without causing any more damage. The few drops of blood he wiped up with a sterile pad and started smoothing the cream over the wound. As he taped a pad in place, he noticed the front of Nash's oversized boxers were tenting out to an impressive level.

He grinned at Nash as he pulled the boxers into place. "Looks like someone's enjoying the attention."

"Give me a break. It's been over a week and I'm horny as hell."

"Really? I figured you'd...."

"Take matters into my own hands? Yeah, well today's the first day I've felt normal." He caught Luke's gaze. "Besides, we needed to talk about some stuff and you've been avoiding it."

Luke's hands slowed and he sighed. "I'm not the only one who has been avoiding our talk. I wanted to wait until you felt better. It's too important to rush." Nash rolled his eyes and Luke couldn't keep from chuckling. "Okay, I'm busted. I was avoiding it."

Loneliness washed over Luke at the thought of losing anyone else he cared for. He tried to assemble his thoughts so he could explain himself to Nash. But when he looked up, the expression on Nash's face was anything but happy.

"It's all right, dude. I get it. It was the whole spur of the moment thing. Don't sweat it. I'm sure I can head out in a day or so. I need to get in touch with my friend Jimmy."

Luke shook his head and waved his hands between them. "Hold on. I didn't change my mind. I'm falling in love with you. Maybe I'm in love with you already, I'm not sure. My perspective isn't that good. But I didn't want to chase you off by looking needy."

Nash's mouth opened and closed several times before his eyebrows scrunched together, and he scowled at Luke. "So all of the sudden the fact that I make my living selling sex isn't a problem?"

Luke considered the question, wanting to say exactly what he intended. "Are you going to keep doing it if we're together?"

His expression turned more severe. "I don't do it for fun, you know."

"Then quit... and move in with me. I need help on the ranch."

"So I'd be your hired guy?"

"We could work out something with money, but I don't sleep with the hired help."

Nash's expression relaxed. "And what about Bobby? He knows who I am."

Luke looked grim and shook his head. "He won't do anything. Especially with what you have on him. He kept us quiet for all those years and was about to crap his pants at the thought that I might do something."

"So. You think it's all going to go perfect now."

This time Luke did smile. "Just because I live out here doesn't mean I'm stupid. Of course we're going to have trouble. Hopefully it won't take another disaster to talk about it."

Nash twisted his face. "I hope I get through the rest of my life without getting shot again. Do you people shoot each other a lot?"

"Almost never. Probably a lot less than get shot in Atlanta."

Nash squinted and studied Luke. After a few tense moments, he nodded in agreement. "I guess so. At least what I almost died over was worth thousands of dollars. Sometimes people get stabbed for twenty bucks."

Luke cupped Nash's face and locked their eyes. "You're worth a lot more than a million bucks. I'd go back with you and find a job in Atlanta if that's what it takes for us to be together."

"You'd leave your ranch and friends to be with me?"

Luke took inventory of his feelings before turning back to Nash. "Yeah, if that's what it takes. I'd sell everything and move with you."

"And what if I told you I didn't want to go back to Atlanta?"

Luke's heart raced at Nash's words. "I would love that. But I know you'd be giving up a lot."

Nash turned and looked out the window before he started. "I grew up on the wrong side of the tracks in a town so small that it barely had tracks. I lost my virginity to a drunk soldier when I was fourteen, was thrown out when my parents found out I was gay, and my dad said if I came back, he'd shoot me."

He turned back to Luke. "Now I look too old for the tricks like Bobby. They might be gross, but at least they don't get off on beating you. The last one didn't have great control. He broke my nose. He likes it rough, and I'll give him what he wants. The last time I was hired, it was him. I didn't know until it was too late, and I ended up in the hospital. With that to go back to, would you be on the first plane to Atlanta?"

Luke stood staring at Nash, trying to find the right words. Nash looked completely forlorn, and he knew he had to speak from the heart. "I want you to stay here. I want to stay here. But whatever we decide, I don't want you to go back to the life you had before."

"Are we just going to be friends? We haven't been together since I was shot."

"Because you were hurt, you dork. I slept on the couch in case you woke up and needed anything."

"You slept in the living room?"

"I knew you wouldn't let me sleep on the floor beside you, I didn't think I could hear you from the master bedroom, and I roll around a lot in bed so I didn't think it would help you getting better."

"You'd sleep on the floor so you could be close?"

Luke smiled and nodded. "Of course. My granddad did it when I was really sick."

Nash gazed at him with a look of amazement etched on his face. He turned and took Luke's hands in his. "How about you help me into our bedroom, and let's have some fun."

Luke started to argue, then smiled broadly when he saw Nash's beaming face. "Sounds like a plan. And I have an idea on how to get you back there in a hurry." Luke scooped Nash in his arms and slowly made his way to the bedroom. After a few steps, Nash wrapped his arms around Luke's neck and leaned against him. They slipped into the dimly lit room, and he gently laid Nash on the bed.

His heart pounded faster as Nash scooted into the middle. He sat on the edge and pulled off his boots and socks and dropped them at the footboard. He crawled to Nash, eased down beside him, and rested his hand against Nash's chest.

"You sure you're up for this? We don't have to do anything if you don't want to."

Nash curled his fingers around Luke's neck and pulled him close. "Shut up, will ya." He pulled them together and pressed their lips tight. Electricity shot from Luke's lips to transform into waves of heat that washed over him. He gave himself over to Nash and focused on the connection they had formed. Nash grabbed Luke's bottom lip with his teeth and tugged for a moment before letting go.

He gazed at Nash, and they both gasped for air. He ran his fingers over Nash's head. "I think you're sexy with short hair."

Nash caressed Luke's face. "You think so? I was so proud of that ponytail."

"Yeah, you look really hot."

Luke slipped his hand down Nash's torso, grabbed his T-shirt, and tugged it over his head. He traced his finger over some of his favorite designs covering his arms and upper chest.

"You think you can deal with a tattooed man in your life? The piercings I could take out, but the tattoos are pretty much permanent."

Luke tugged gently on the ring going through one of Nash's nipples and was rewarded with a groan. "You leave everything right where it is. The uptight people around here will have to get over the whole tattoo thing. It was illegal here until a few years ago, so it's still kind of unique."

"Glad to hear it, or we might have had our first problem as a couple."

Luke leaned down and flicked his tongue over Nash's hard nipple. "No problem on my end. Give me a chance to figure out what you like."

"Don't worry. I'll tell you."

Luke ran his fingers over Nash's chest as they kissed again. He circled his navel slowly and followed the almost invisible trail of blond hair that disappeared into the elastic waistband of his shorts. Sliding them lower, he found Nash's hard shaft and began jacking it slowly through the shorts.

"That thing's hard as iron."

"It usually doesn't go this long without relief. You keep that up and it's going to go off."

Luke tightened his grip, leaned closer to Nash, and flicked his tongue over his nipple again. "Would that be so bad?"

Nash was beginning to pant and his eyes rolled back. "No. It's all good."

Luke toyed with it for another minute or two before releasing the nipple. Nash's breath hissed between his teeth. "Ah, shit. You've got me all boned up."

He moved lower, grabbed Nash's shorts, and eased them down his legs. He took his time working them over the still healing wound, and at one point he thought he heard a tiny gasp from Nash. He tossed them to the floor and turned to see his love grinning at him, his hands behind his head and his cock sticking straight up.

Luke stood and quickly stripped, his clothes adding to the pile on the floor. He crawled between Nash's legs. They opened farther while Luke ran his hands over them. He leaned in and kissed the phoenix tattoo on Nash's shin. Careful to avoid the leg injury, Luke licked and kissed his way upward, his senses filled with the smells and tastes of the man under him. The moans coming from Nash left no doubt as to the success of what he was doing.

He wriggled higher and flicked his tongue just under Nash's nuts. The volume of groans increased with each pass of his tongue, until his balls were sucked tight against the shaft.

"Wait, stop. I'm about to lose it."

Luke leaned in, kissed just below the crimson head, and sat back on his heels to enjoy the results of his work. Nash's entire body was flushed, his fists clenched in the sheets and his breath coming in gasps.

"So, how was that?"

"Oh, shit. Any more and I'm going to shoot. Give me a minute."

Luke moved close again and kissed Nash's slit. Nash gritted his teeth and let out a guttural sound. A stream of clear precome ran down its length. Even knowing he was so close, Luke couldn't help but caress the almost hairless skin on Nash's legs.

Nash pushed himself onto his elbows and grinned at Luke. "You're wanting to make sure I unload, aren't you? You need to come up here where you can do less damage. Besides, I want some of what's jutting out from between your legs."

Luke carefully crawled free and knelt beside Nash. He pressed his hardness down and bounced the spongy head against Nash's open mouth. Nash grabbed Luke's cock and slowly jacked it.

"This thing could keep a man satisfied for his whole life."

Heat raced over Luke at the words, and Nash washed his tongue around the rim. The sensation coming from his cock left Luke wanting more. He swung a leg over and pressed himself into Nash's mouth. Nash slid his hands around Luke's hips, grabbed his buttcheeks, and pulled him closer. Luke groaned as he slid into Nash's throat, and his eyes fluttered closed as Nash's lips brushed against the bulge. Luke pulled him tight against his crotch.

"Holy fuck."

Nash bobbed his head once, then came off Luke's stiff cock. He panted heavily while continuing to stroke it.

"I thought you were too nice to say such things."

"Oh hell, you're going to hear a lot more before it's over. Keep doing that." Luke pressed forward as Nash opened his mouth again. Soon he was thrusting between hot lips as he lost himself in the heat of Nash's mouth.

Nash slipped his fingers closer and slid them up and down the crack of Luke's ass while sucking his dick. Luke knew his orgasm was building, but he wasn't ready to finish so quickly. He wanted something new this time. Luke pulled his aching cock out and sat on Nash's flat stomach, careful to avoid the shallow cut on his side. He grinned at Nash as he worked to regain control. "I want to get fucked. You think you're up for that?"

Nash grabbed Luke's nipples and tugged on them. "I can pound your ass until Chris will hear you at her house, cowboy." Nash curled to sit up, and a grimace flashed across his face.

"What's wrong?"

"Nothing. But we might need to work on how this is going to happen."

Luke kissed Nash and caressed his face. "Let's wait. It's not like we aren't going to have time."

"Oh, hell no. I'm fucking you today."

Luke chuckled again. "It's not like you haven't screwed me before. I'm up for it."

Nash wrapped his arms around Luke and pulled him into a tight hug. The comfort that flowed from Nash was the most affection Luke could remember in years. Internal barricades that he'd had since junior high melted away like snow on a hot summer day. Nash kissed him between his pecs and Luke's cock tightened even more.

Nash looked at him with eyes so green that Luke could lose himself in them for days. "I know what you've had before. I plan to make you feel amazing again. But first we got to get you ready. Where's your jack-off juice?"

A glimmer of embarrassment flickered through Luke, but he knew this bluntness was part of what he loved about Nash. "There's a little bottle in the side table, and a big bottle in the bathroom if we need it."

Nash squirmed over and pulled out the drawer before Luke had time to think about it. And Nash started laughing. "For such a good boy, you got a lot of sex toys."

Luke's face blazed with fire at being discovered. "It's not that bad."

Nash held up a purple jelly dildo and chuckled. "Maybe we won't need as much prep time as I thought."

Luke bristled before deflating with a sigh. He rolled his eyes and grinned. "I guess I do have a few toys. Looks like I won't need them anymore."

"Oh hell no. Toys by yourself are fun, toys with someone else can be mind-blowing." Nash grinned at Luke. "So I'm guessing your collection of porn is pretty impressive too?"

"Oh, shut it or you ain't tapping anything tonight."

Nash's smile got even wider. He slapped Luke on the thigh. "Get your hot ass off me and onto your hands and knees. We've got some work to do."

Luke carefully moved beside Nash and did as he was instructed. Nash slipped behind him, popped open the bottle of lube, and drizzled a thin stream down Luke's crack.

"Shit. That's cold."

Nash pressed his fingers down the cleft and smeared lube over his ass. The slick, hot fingers forced a groan from deep inside him. He dropped his chest to the bed and closed his eyes as the sensations washed over him. Nash's touch inched like a fire over his skin until it found its goal. He pressed against Luke's opening a few times before slipping the tip inside.

"Holy fuck. So good."

"Oh just wait, stud. It's gonna get much better."

Nash worked slowly, occasionally adding more lube, until his knuckles bumped against Luke's ass. His finger found that spot deep inside Luke, and he about shot his load.

"Oh God. Oh shit. I love it when you hit that spot."

"Just a little gift inside you. Looks like yours is good and sensitive." He wiggled his finger inside Luke again. This time the wash of sensations left Luke shaking.

"Keep that up and we'll be done in about a minute."

Nash chuckled and pulled his finger out. Gasping for air and working for control, Luke barely noticed when Nash applied more lube and slipped two fingers inside him. He groaned and reached for his cock, but Nash knocked his hand away.

"Oh no you don't. You aren't getting off without me being buried in your ass."

Luke groaned and twisted his hands in the sheet as the waves of euphoria washed over him. He relaxed as Nash slowly opened him. Before long he was pressing back against Nash's fingers. He glanced over his shoulder to see an intent look on Nash's face.

"You're killing me. Fuck me already. Goddamn, I need fucked."

Nash chuckled as he buried the fingers deep inside and slowly rotated them in Luke's ass. "Well you get plumb potty-mouthed when you have something in your butt."

"If you don't hurry up and fuck me, I swear I'll use the damn purple dildo."

Nash pulled his fingers out and landed a stinging slap on Luke's ass to fan the fire to higher levels. Nash eased himself onto the bed and lay with his cock sticking almost straight up. He grabbed a condom from the drawer and unrolled it onto his dick.

"So here's how this is going down. You're going to get all the dick you can handle, but you're going to be doing the work."

Luke grinned and asked, "You mean cowboy position?"

"We going to fuck, or are you going to sit around and giggle?"

"We can't do both?"

"Only if I'm a much worse lover than I think I am," Nash said. "Now, get over here."

Luke carefully swung his leg over Nash and eased himself down to his stomach. As Nash's hard shaft slipped between his asscheeks, any thoughts but what they were about to do left his head. Automatically he rocked his hips back and forth, enjoying the sensations. His cock grew hard, aching, and he was ready.

He reached back, grabbed Nash's cock, and slipped it down his crack. The spongy head sank into his opening. He pressed downward until he began to stretch and stopped. "Damn. You're harder than the toys."

"I'd hope so. But take it easy. You don't want to hurt yourself."

Luke nodded, continuing to work his way deeper, until with a slight shove, Nash slipped inside him. He dropped his head as he slumped forward to catch himself on Nash's chest. His body was covered with a sheen of sweat, and he fought to keep from panting.

Nash reached up and ran his hands over Luke's chest, tugging at his nipples as he did. "Relax, it gets better. Give it a minute."

"Shit. Feels amazing. Just need a sec." He began pressing and rocking as Nash slipped deeper and deeper inside him. The sensation was amazing, and the faint pain was soon overwhelmed by the

175

pleasure that radiated from his center. His body slowly relaxed as he sat panting above Nash.

Nash ran his hands over Luke again, flicking his nipples and rubbing his fingers over his chest. Luke shifted his weight and slid back and forth. The sensation of Nash's thick cock grinding inside him was cranking up the passion to a new level. Nash grabbed his thighs and thrust into him. Luke leaned backward, and fireworks shot through his body.

"Fuck!"

"Lean back more."

When he did, Nash plowed against Luke's prostate and he sent out a blob of clear gel that formed a stream making its way down his cock. He was lost in the sensation, his dick hard and waving over him as he rocked harder while the pleasure filled his body. Nash bounced inside him and the familiar tingle built in his crotch.

No longer able to string words together, Luke's groans of pleasure increased in volume as he reached the edge and hovered at it. He desperately needed release but couldn't seem to reach that level. Nash pounded him, keeping him teetering on this side of climax. He reached up, grabbed Luke's nipples, and tugged on them. The sweet mixture of pain and ecstasy sent Luke over the edge. With a tremble his body locked and his cock swelled harder than Luke could have imagined as he shot the first strand of white.

Luke convulsed again and again as the built-up pressure sought release. With a final teeth-grinding contraction, the last pool of come oozed from Luke and into a crisscross of translucent white that covered Nash's pale skin. He slowly came to a stop and smiled at Nash.

"Apparently it was quite a while for me too. I never remember shooting like that before."

Nash ran his fingers through the thickest pool, smearing it through the hair on Luke's chest. He trailed his fingers through Luke's bush, wrapped the semen-coated lengths around his softening cock, and toyed with it. He leaned forward until their lips met, and they shared a kiss that left him tingling. Luke sat up and ran his hands over Nash.

"Your turn. How do you want me?" Luke asked.

"On your back. I plan on pounding your ass."

Luke rolled them over and groaned as Nash sank deep inside him. He rocked back and forth, enjoying the sensations of Nash's hard cock. After a moment he shot him a lecherous grin. "Go for it, stud. Give me what you got."

Nash pulled Luke close and began kissing passionately as he started pile driving into Luke. Soon they broke the kiss as Nash focused only on releasing himself. He enjoyed the lusty thrusts and could tell Nash wasn't going to last long. They moved together as Nash neared his climax. Luke found he was enjoying the intimacy.

"Oh God. Oh damn!" Nash pinned himself against Luke as he orgasmed. Luke relaxed and enjoyed the expressions of pleasure that flowed across Nash's face. Their bodies mashed against each other as Nash was lost in the depths of his orgasm. As he slowly sank into the bed, Luke lay across him and they kissed gently. They lost track of time as they cuddled until Nash slipped out of bed.

Luke rose, his eyebrows knotted together. "Hmm, Nash."

Nash came up on his elbows. "What's wrong? Did I hurt you?"

"Hmm, well. You know I've only bottomed once before."

"Yeah, I know. What is it? Tell me."

"I'm shaking like crazy…."

Nash looked at him with concern and broke into a smirk. "Yeah, that happens. I was banging your prostate pretty good. Let's go shower and clean you up before we crash."

Luke nodded and made his way carefully to the bathroom. Nash followed him as he adjusted the glass-walled shower. He shuddered when Nash ran his hand over his ass cheek and teased his opening. When a few fingers slipped inside, Luke caught himself on the shower wall and moaned.

"I love that I pounded you until your ass is all hungry and sucking my fingers in."

Luke pulled Nash into a kiss, then led him into the shower. He wrapped his arms around Nash and held him tight. "I never imagined it would feel so good. I thought my head would explode."

"Well as much man juice as you hit me with, I'd guess your nuts look like raisins." Nash dropped his hand between Luke's legs and grabbed his sac. "Nope, still nice healthy egg size."

Another shiver ran through Luke and his cock filled for a second round. "Okay, enough with the testicular exams. I'm hard again, and we've probably already done more than your leg wanted."

Nash twisted his lips and looked down at his leg. "Yeah, you're probably right. It's likely not as healed as I'd like to think."

Luke chuckled and filled his hand with soap. "Come on, let's get cleaned up. And you keep your fingers out of my butt." He worked the thick lather over Nash and was rewarded with small sighs when he rubbed his hands over Nash's nipples. When he reached Nash's face, he held it as their gazes locked. "I want you to stay here. I don't want you to go back."

"I don't want to go back either. Even if the fucking rednecks shoot me around here."

"Just to point out, Koslov isn't from here." Luke felt a surge of orneriness. "Any local would've been carrying a bigger gun than a .38."

"Thanks, that makes me feel a whole lot better."

"Close your mouth and your eyes." Luke gently washed Nash's face, enjoying the time to check him out. The stubble on his cheeks gave Luke a warm feeling that traveled through him. Luke traced over his face until Nash shuddered. He slipped his hands to Nash's shoulder and rubbed his fingers over his tense muscles. Luke guided Nash back under the warm water to help rinse off the soap.

Nash grinned as he stepped from under the stream and pushed the water from his face with his hands. "My turn."

Nash filled his palm with soap and started working it over Luke's hair-covered chest. His touch felt delicious as it slid across his torso, teasing his hard nipples. Nash turned him so he was pinned against the glass wall and began soaping his back. Luke closed his eyes and enjoyed the touch.

As Nash coated his buttcheeks with lather, he sighed and spread his legs wider. Luke became lost in the feelings but eventually Nash was finishing with each of his feet, and he was as hard as flint again. He followed Nash's gentle guidance until he'd turned back to face his love.

"Yummy. I think you need another round."

Luke grabbed his shoulders and kept him standing. "It's okay. I'll survive not getting off twice. I don't want you to open the wound."

Nash wrapped his fingers tightly around Luke's cock and stroked him. "Ever shot off in the shower?"

"Yeah, sure."

"Ever shot off in the shower with someone else jerking you off?"

The sensations built quickly as Luke swallowed hard and shook his head.

"Well, this is going to be a day of fun for you, isn't it?" With that he pulled Luke against him, reached around, and grabbed his hard cock. The sensation of Nash enveloping him made him feel truly loved for the first time since losing his grandparents. The sense of contentment was met with an equally strong wave of euphoria. Luke leaned against Nash as his hand started him toward his second climax of the night.

He was winding his way closer to an orgasm when Nash ran his hand over Luke's nipples. The electric jolts that ran through his body added to the pleasure. One of his secret wishes had always been to be taller, but in this moment with Nash holding him, he was glad they fit the way they did.

The dual assault on his senses sent him closer. His body tensed and his orgasm began. The delicious sensations continued as he emptied himself for a second time. As the last of his semen dripped onto the floor to be washed away, he twisted in Nash's arms and stretched up for a kiss.

"That was amazing. But you didn't have to do that. You were the horny one."

Nash chuckled after returning Luke's kiss. "Fair warning, I'm going to want to have sex with you a lot. And that little drawer is never going to hold all our toys."

Luke turned off the water and lifted Nash in his arms. "Sounds fucking excellent to me."

EPILOGUE

Six Months Later

KEYS WERE jingling in the front door in a way that was far too familiar to Nash. He shook Luke. "Chris is here. I thought you were getting the key back."

"Luke! Nash! Get your sweet asses up. You won't believe what happened."

"Why didn't I get that key? Damn." Luke pulled the pillow over his head and moaned.

"Come on, get up. Surely the sex should be getting less interesting at this point. Get up."

Nash threw the blankets off himself and stretched, his naked body wriggling across the bed. He pulled them off Luke too, pausing to enjoy the fresh ink on Luke's shoulder. He had a matching one on his leg around the gunshot scar. Exact duplicates of two koi, one gold and one blue, swimming around their initials. The initials were a compromise; Luke had wanted their names, but Nash had convinced him that putting your lover's name on you was a curse on the relationship.

"Goddammit! Get! Up!"

Nash sat up and snagged the jeans he'd dropped on the floor last night. Regardless of what Chris thought, sex between the two of them was hotter than ever. Once Luke believed Nash was open to exploring new things in their sex life, he became insatiable. But Nash didn't mind. Actually, he loved Luke's newfound enthusiasm.

Nash stood and pulled the jeans up, tucking himself in them before zipping them. He looked over to see Luke had stopped moving again. He crawled across the bed and swatted his bare asscheek.

181

Luke yelped and jumped away, rubbing his butt. "Hey. What was that for?"

"Get your ass up. Can't you hear her?"

Nash grinned at the handprint on Luke's ass as he stood and stretched. It changed to chuckling when he turned and his morning wood was sticking straight out in front of him. "You better get him in a pair of jeans before she walks in here to see what's taking so long."

Luke grumbled but moved to slip into his jeans. His erection didn't make getting into his pants any easier, but he managed, leaving a thick bulge for Nash to enjoy. He followed Nash's stare and pulled on a T-shirt. Once he got on the shirt and adjusted it to hide his hard cock, he waved Nash ahead of him. "Go on. Let's see what crisis has her worked up enough to wake us up this time."

They walked into the room and found Chris pacing back and forth with one of their coffee cups in her hands. Nash caught the scent of fresh coffee and went in to pour himself a cup. He walked back in as Luke got himself a glass of milk and sprawled into one of the new leather chairs that he and Luke had picked out.

Nash took a seat as Chris paced frantically. But even though she seemed about to burst, she waited until Luke had settled onto the couch.

"You will *not* believe what's happened." Chris vibrated with nervous energy.

Luke's jaws seemed able to unhinged with a massive yawn as he turned to Chris. "What's got you so excited? It's awfully early."

"Oh my God, before you found regular sex you would have already been at work for an hour. Now with you two and your hot monkey love, it's a miracle if you're up by seven thirty."

"Yeah, yeah. We have sex all the time. No news there. What's up?" Nash asked.

A look of tremendous satisfaction colored Chris's face. "Guess who is in jail in Missouri?"

"Your cousin Mike?" Luke asked.

"He's been out of jail for several months now. And hopefully will get his license back soon, smartass. No, your best buddy."

Luke's eyebrow shot up as he watched Chris dancing in place. "Who? For God's sake, you're enjoying this more than the time Bobby got busted for having beer in his car in high school."

Nash's head popped up, and he focused on the conversation. "Bobby. It's Bobby isn't it? It all finally caught up with him."

"Yes, oh my God it all hit the fan at once," Chris said.

Luke leaned toward his friend, his hands clenching his glass. "Come on. Spill it."

"They had a sexual predator sting in Springfield. Bobby thought he was meeting some thirteen-year-old boy whose parents were gone for the weekend. But no, he met with several nice burly cops who were more than happy to give him the royal treatment."

Luke looked at Chris and then Nash. "It's like you said. He could only get it up for boys." Nash kept his silence and gave Luke time to think through what this meant to him. He looked at Chris. "What about his family? His kids?"

"Yeah, that's the bad thing. But apparently Aimee had already had the paperwork for a divorce with her lawyer. So things weren't rosy at home."

"Shit, he screwed up everything. I almost feel bad for him."

"I don't. Son of a bitch got what he deserved," Nash said.

Luke shook his head and Nash could see the warring emotions inside him. Before the feelings twisted Luke into knots, he pulled them together. "Wasn't anything you did or didn't do. He's getting what's coming to him. So stop worrying about it. He went to have sex with an eighth grader. Whatever he gets, he deserves."

"A lifetime on a sexual predator list in Missouri."

Luke spun back to Chris. "What?"

"I don't know what all he's been charged with, but in Missouri he's on the sex offenders list for life if they find him guilty of any of a long list of things."

"Man, he's fucked up his life. What an idiot," Nash said.

"He thought he was bulletproof. Everybody here thought he was God's gift and didn't notice anything else."

"I noticed. But no one cares about a homeless gay kid," Nash said.

"I was even dumber than I thought. He was doing God knows what with God knows who while I thought I was too strange because…." He looked at Chris. "Anyway, he made me think I wasn't worth much. Then he dropped me like a bag of shit. That was a great feeling."

Nash pulled Luke against him and kissed the side of his neck. "He was a fucking idiot, and you're stuck with me for a long time."

Luke turned and wrapped Nash into a tight hug. He could feel Luke tremble in his arms. Chris made her way to the kitchen, pulled out a couple of skillets, and rummaged through the refrigerator.

When she looked at them again, the pair hadn't moved much. "Hey, if you two are going to have sex, why don't you film it for me. That'd save me some cash buying the hot cowboy sex films online."

Luke chuckled as he released Nash and gave him a tender kiss. Then he turned toward Chris. "Nope, you can pay for it just like we do. Now what the heck are you dragging out? I'm the one taking the culinary classes, even if it was to make sure Nash didn't run off with any of the cute art students from his classes at Northeastern."

Nash smiled as the two of them bickered like an old married couple. But he knew who he'd fallen in love with. Even if falling for a cowboy was the oldest story in the book.

JON KEYS's earliest memories revolve around books. Either read to him or making up stories based on the illustrations, these were places his active mind occupied. As he got older, the selection expanded beyond Mother Goose and Dr. Seuss to the world of westerns, science fiction, and fantasy. His world filled with dragon riders, mind-speaking horses, and comic book heroes in hot uniforms.

A voracious reader for half a century, Jon recently began creating his own fiction. The first writing was his attempt at showing rural characters in a more sympathetic light. Now he has moved into some of the writing he lost himself in for so many years—fantasy. Jon has worked as a ranch hand, teacher, computer tech, roughneck, designer, retail clerk, welder, artist, and, yes, pool boy; with interests ranging from kayaking and hunting to drawing and cooking, he uses this range of life experiences to create written works that draw the reader in and wrap them in a good story.

E-mail: jon.keys@ymail.com
Blog: jonkeys.com
Facebook: www.facebook.com/jon.keys.773
Twitter: @Jon4Keys

HOME GROWN

Jon Keys

Peter Stevens believes nothing tastes better than a vine-ripened tomato tended by a farmer's hands. The craving for heirloom tomatoes leads him to his local farmers' market and his favorite vendor, Ethan Hart. As Peter becomes a regular customer, the two find they have more in common than a love of good food. Just as Ethan begins to relax, Peter's ex, Jay, appears and is all the things Ethan is not. A perfect storm of mistakes and poor choices, as well as Ethan's haunted past, has him ready to admit defeat. With the guidance of friends and a goat far too smart for her own good, Ethan realizes he needs to have a tender hand and patience to grow a home for Peter.

www.dreamspinnerpress.com

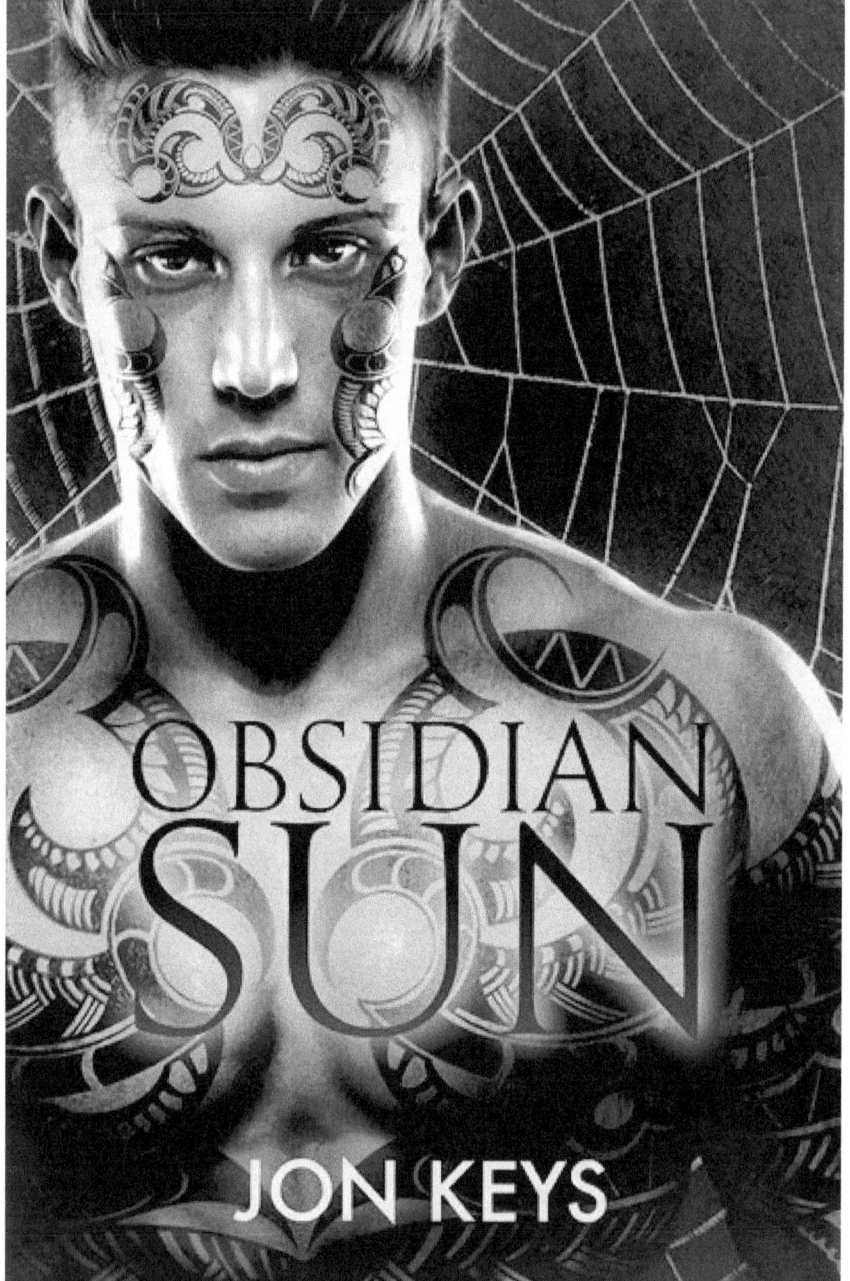

OBSIDIAN SUN

JON KEYS

Obsidian Series: Book One

Differences must be put aside when vengeance becomes all-consuming.

Anan, a spellweaver of the Talac people, returns from a hunting trip to find his village decimated, his mate dead, and everyone else captured by Varas slavers. The sole survivor is Terja, a young man without the velvet that covers most Talac, marking him as a spellspinner. Since Talac magic requires both a weaver and a spinner, Anan and Terja must move beyond their ingrained mistrust. All that remains is revenge and a desperate plan to rescue their tribesmen before they are sold to Varas pleasure houses. A goal Anan and Terja are willing to die for.

With the blessing of the Talac gods, they discover new and surprising ways to complement each other's power. But as they race through terrain full of enemies and dangerous creatures to reach their people before they pass into Varas lands, they must take drastic steps to face the overwhelming odds against them. Understanding their connection might be their only hope.

www.dreamspinnerpress.com

OBSIDIAN
MOONS

JON KEYS

Sequel to *Obsidian Sun*
Obsidian Series: Book Two

After achieving the impossible and releasing their people from the Varas slavers, Anan and Terja, a spellweaver and spellspinner, start the arduous journey back to their homeland. A winter trek across the grasslands is dangerous enough, but the traitor, Xain, is tasked with recapturing the slaves, and failure will mean his death. As added insurance, the Varas High Regent hires a Triad of legendary Ubica assassins and assigns a full regiment of his personal guards, along with their captain, to the task. Their mission is clear: recapture the escaped Talac slaves destined for the Varas pleasure houses—and the bed of the High Regent—at any cost.

The newly freed Talac travel toward their homelands with the full knowledge they are likely being pursued. The flight westward is fraught with new and unexpected dangers as Anan and Terja struggle to save their tribe. The battle for shelter, food, and a way to defend themselves becomes an all-consuming task, but they are reminded by the avatars of their gods that all is not as it appears.

www.dreamspinnerpress.com

Also from Dreamspinner Press

The Release Series

CATCH AND
RELEASE

BA Tortuga

Also from Dreamspinner Press

COWBOYS DON'T
COME OUT

TARA LAIN

www.dreamspinnerpress.com

www.ingramcontent.com/pod-product-compliance
Lightning Source LLC
Chambersburg PA
CBHW060057260626
47160CB00005B/1701